Counselor

by
Dave Aquino

CCB Publishing
British Columbia, Canada

Counselor

Copyright ©2004, 2013 by Dave Aquino
ISBN-13   978-1-77143-056-2
Second Edition

Library and Archives Canada Cataloguing in Publication
Aquino, Dave, 1981-
Counselor / written by Dave Aquino.
ISBN 978-1-77143-056-2
Also available in electronic format.
Additional cataloguing data available from Library and Archives Canada

Cover artwork: Man wearing sunglasses: © RTimages | Canstockphoto.com
Gun in hand: © Elnur | Canstockphoto.com

Extreme care has been taken by the author to ensure that all information presented in this book is accurate and up to date at the time of publishing. Neither the author nor the publisher can be held responsible for any errors or omissions. Additionally, neither is any liability assumed for damages resulting from the use of the information contained herein.

Publisher: CCB Publishing
             British Columbia, Canada
             www.ccbpublishing.com

Contents

Chapter 1: Shot in the Dark 1

Chapter 2: Jack Reddick 11

Chapter 3: The New Lead 20

Chapter 4: Junkyard Anger 28

Chapter 5: The Wrong Turn 40

Chapter 6: The New Problem 48

Chapter 7: The Trial 57

Chapter 8: Ted's Story Begins 67

Chapter 9: Claudia 76

Chapter 10: Trouble in the Family 83

Chapter 11: Breaking the News 90

Chapter 12: Getting Everything I Want 96

Chapter 13: Feeling Good 102

Chapter 14: Counselor 105

Chapter 15: Finding Ann 117

Chapter 16: Ted's Story Ends 128

Chapter 17: Jack's Recovery 129

Chapter 1

Shot in the Dark

It was November 8, 1999. That morning, Charlie took his wedding ring to a nearby pawnshop.

"I guess I don't need this ring anymore," Charlie said.

Ted waited in the Cadillac until Charlie came out with a bag in his hand.

"What's in there?" Ted asked.

"Supplies."

Charlie handed Ted a handheld walkie-talkie. Ted noticed something else big in the bag.

"Are you sure we want to pay Peggy a visit today?" Charlie asked.

"Yes, I need to."

Both of them drove to the school; Ted parked near the main entrance.

"Be careful in there," Charlie said.

"Listen for me on the walkie-talkie and, well, you know," Ted said.

"Yeah, I know, I'll listen for you."

Ted went inside the school while Charlie stayed in the running car. Ted's mirrored sunglasses and Army helmet got the attention of a teacher who was in the hallway with some students. Mrs. Lipan gave this six-foot tall man in his forties, looking like GI Joe, a weird look. Ted paid no attention to the short old wrinkling lady with thin gray hair.

"Can I help you sir?" she asked.

Ted kept walking towards the counseling office, still ignoring her completely. Mrs. Lipan followed him from a distance. He reached the counseling office and approached the secretary.

"Could I speak to the school counselor, Mrs. Reddick?" Ted asked.

Mrs. Lipan didn't think much of this man now. She figured he was one of the student's fathers, but still watched, just to be sure.

"Are you a parent?" the secretary asked.

"Yes, I'll wait in the hallway for her; just send her out," Ted replied.

After five minutes, Peggy came out, a bit disturbed inside, by the man in the Army helmet and mirrored sunglasses. Yet, she still had a stupid little grin on her face, along with a mineral water in her hand.

"Did you want to see me, sir?" Peggy asked.

"Ohhhh, yes," Ted said with a deep, almost psychotic voice and a dead-on stare.

"And who are you?" Peggy Reddick asked, with a snotty little tone.

Ted smiled and took off the sunglasses and helmet to get a better look at Peggy. Even though her bleached blonde hair was in pig-tails instead of curled and parted in the middle the way he remembered, Ted knew it was she. Her being a middle-aged six-foot tall woman with a big butt and huge sagging chest easily gave her away. Ted looked directly into her blue eyes, with his wide crazy eyes and a sharp evil smile on his face. It took Peggy a moment or two to realize who he was. She dropped her water at the sight of this man.

"Oh, my God! Oh, my God! Oh, my God! What do you want?" Peggy screamed.

The look on her face was so thunderstruck, even Ted couldn't believe it. She would sooner have expected the President than this man. She thought she had outsmarted Ted and would never have to deal with what she did to him. It hit home completely without delay. She was hoping it was either a look-alike, or a dream. Her body froze in fear, yet, she didn't think Ted would have the gall to do anything in the middle of a public school in broad daylight.

"Oh, so you remember me? I figured you would," Ted said.

He whipped out his .45 handgun. Blam! He shot her in the chest.

"That one's for me."

Blam! He shot her again.

"That one's for Charlie."

Blam! He shot her again.

"That one's for anyone else you fucked over."

Mrs. Lipan ran to the security office to get help. Peggy was on the ground, bleeding badly, choking on her own blood.

"You'll never get away with this," Peggy said with a dry voice.

"Wrong."

Ted pulled out the walkie-talkie and yelled, "Charlie, this is it!" The over-confident unarmed security guard and Mrs. Lipan were running towards Ted, who still had the smoking gun in his hand. The guard thought it would be an easy arrest, since the man wasn't even trying to run. The guard was twenty feet away when a huge noise came from behind them. They turned around to see Charlie crashed the Cadillac through the front doors. The guard and Mrs. Lipan stopped running towards Ted and into a nearby classroom to avoid getting hit. Ted ran towards the car. Charlie slowed down just enough so Ted could get in. Peggy looked up, with what little strength she had. The last thing she saw was the massive grille of the Cadillac, as it smashed her face into the floor, killing her instantly.

Ted and Charlie drove though a pair of glass double doors leading outside. After going through the football field, they were back on the road. The car has some body damage from driving through the school, but was running fine. They turned on their police scanner.

"Attention, all units, we just had shots fired at the school. Look for an old 70's Cadillac with some body damage on it," dispatch said over the scanner.

While this was going on, a local cop named John Marshall was on break, talking to his friend Randy Casner about an old case.

"I still can't believe we never got a chance to put ole' William Defreno away," Marshall said.

"Yeah, well, I still wanna know where that money went," Randy said.

"Oh, yes, are you gonna be ready for court? Remember what I

told you," Marshall said.

"Yes, I'm not worried," Randy said with a laugh. Marshall laughed as well. As they were talking, Marshall's emergency radio came on.

"Marshall, look for an old beat up 70's Cadillac. Two guys are in it; they just committed a murder at the middle school. I've informed Officer's Bundy and Rosen," Dispatch said.

"Oh, my, well they sure picked the wrong town to mess with," Marshall said to Randy.

"Go kill 'em John; nobody commits a murder in my town and gets away with it," Randy said.

Marshall got on his motorcycle, drove up the road to the main street of the city. To his surprise, he saw the beat up Cadillac going about forty miles per hour, a good distance away. Marshall drew his gun and aimed it towards the car. Charlie saw Marshall and hit the nitrous booster. The Cadillac went from forty miles per hour to seventy-five miles per hour in only seconds, because of the nitrous. Marshall fired two shots through the windshield, but didn't hit either of the two men. He saw the car getting closer and going extremely fast.

"Oh, shit!" Marshall screamed.

He revved his bike and tried to get away, but it didn't work. Charlie aimed the car at Marshall, smashing into him on his bike at eighty-five miles per hour. Marshall's head hit the hood as he fell onto the street. Charlie slammed on the brakes and took a sharp right, heading towards the Interstate.

"Oh, God, why?" Marshall said out loud before he died in the middle of the street.

Officer's Bundy and Rosen were in their squad car trying to raise Marshall on the radio. Finally, they found Marshall in the road, and called for an ambulance.

"Bundy and Rosen, I called for an ambulance. There's one already being sent to the middle school; I'm going to contact the State Police," Dispatch said.

Rosen picked up the CB.

"Absolutely not; we don't need the Smokies. Me and Bundy are gonna gut those sons of bitches ourselves," Rosen said to Dispatch.

"But Rosen, we need to call the State Police," dispatch said.

Rosen was mad now.

"Are you deaf? Or just stupid? Don't call the State Police. They get enough credit for this shit; we'll get 'em ourselves."

Peggy's husband Jack Reddick was called. He got to the school when the ambulance arrived. Since he was a Sergeant detective in the next city over, he could join the chase. Being a typical suburban man, he loved the power of the police cars. His personal vehicle, an economy car, always bogged down on steep hills.

Anyone could see he was a cop by the clean-cut black hair, the typical cop mustache, and being 6' 2" with 185 pounds of muscle on him. Jack was only forty-two, but the lines on his face easily made him look fifty or older.

"Oh, God, is she gonna be okay?" Jack Reddick asked the paramedics.

"We'll see what we can do," one said, reluctant to tell him the truth. "Why don't you get in your police car and try to catch these guys? The city cops here could really use your help."

"I'm not gonna leave my wife here," Jack Reddick said.

"Really, there's nothing you can do; she's already dead. All you can do is catch these guys."

Jack knew the paramedics were right. He kissed his wife goodbye as they loaded her into the ambulance, and got in his police car to find these guys.

"Officer's Bundy and Rosen, this is Jack Reddick, do you read?" Jack said into the radio.

"Yes, are you gonna help us?" Rosen asked.

"Yes."

"Where do you think they are?"

"I'd say they headed towards the Interstate," Jack replied.

"Copy."

Rosen, Bundy and Jack headed towards the Interstate with their lights flashing, going over one hundred miles per hour.

"We're gonna get an ambulance to Officer Marshall soon. Peggy Reddick is checked in to the hospital," Dispatch said.

"Take your time. Marshall's dead; I'm sure of it," Rosen said.

Rosen, Bundy and Jack caught up to Ted and Charlie.

"Oh, they caught up to us," Ted said.

Charlie hit the nitrous booster again. The jolt of energy brought them up to one hundred twenty miles per hour on the Interstate. Within a few minutes, the two squad cars caught up again.

"Look in the bag," Charlie said.

Ted looked, to see that Charlie had bought a 12-gauge shotgun at the pawnshop. He opened the box of ammo and loaded it. Bundy and Rosen's car got right up beside the Cadillac. Since Bundy was in the passenger seat, he rolled down his window and fired aimlessly. The high speeds and adrenaline made it hard to get an accurate shot. Bundy shot out the back driver's side window and the back windshield of the Cadillac in him aimless shooting. Ted shot back at them with the shotgun. Rosen backed off and swerved the car behind them. Rosen's car and Jack's car got on each side of the Cadillac.

They sandwiched the car and started to slow it down. The Cadillac was stuck to Rosen's car from them pressing up against each other. Rosen slammed his brakes; since the Cadillac was stuck to his car, both cars slowed down. Jack got behind the Cadillac to ram it. Rosen's car slowed Ted and Charlie down to fifty-five miles per hour. Charlie drove the Cadillac with Rosen's car attached, over the median to the wrong side of the road. The Cadillac was in the shoulder, but Rosen's car was on a head-on collision course with oncoming traffic. Charlie saw an RV headed toward them. Charlie aimed the car just right, so that Rosen's car would be in the path of destruction.

Crash!! The RV crashed into Rosen's car and the car broke away, taking the front fender of the Cadillac with it. Charlie crossed the median, back to the right side of the road.

The Cadillac had three busted windows, bullet holes, and was missing a fender. The engine was heating up fast, with loud knocking noises coming from it. Ted and Charlie knew they could blow the engine any second. Being rid of one police car brought no relief, because they still had Jack's car to worry about. Jack went to where Rosen and Bundy had crashed. Amazingly they were not hurt real bad.

"Get in, Rosen," Jack said.

"I'll drive; get over," Rosen replied.

Rosen and Jack floored the police cruiser to its limits. Once again, they caught up to Ted and Charlie.

"Did you guys call the State Police?" Jack asked.

"Yeah, they should be here soon," Rosen answered nervously.

Rosen was lying; no state police were coming. He and Bundy had thought they could handle it alone. He remembered a case where he caught the bank robbers, but the State Police got all the fame and glory for it. He swore not to let it happen again. Jack took out his handgun and shot out the passenger side window of the Cadillac. The window broke and he saw the passenger go down. For a moment, Jack thought he'd shot the man dead, but then he saw him get up again. The glass had shattered in Ted's face, leaving him cut, but all in all, not badly hurt. Jack and Rosen got behind the car, hoping to hit it on the tail light, and spin it out of control. Before they could, Charlie slammed the brakes, locking the tires.

Wham! The police car hit the back of the Cadillac directly. Since the Cadillac was heavier, it did more damage to Jack's car. The front grille of the police car was smashed, with water and smoke coming from the engine. Rosen and Jack knew they'd broken the radiator, and didn't have much time before the car would overheat. They floored the police car again and side-swiped the Cadillac in a panicked last ditch attempt to stop these guys.

"Ted, we got one more nitrous boost," Charlie said. "Are you ready?"

"Yes, I'm gonna shoot their car, and as soon as I do, slam it!" Ted replied.

Jack got the shotgun from the rear rack and eased his body out the window. Ted eased his body out of the Cadillac's window with a shotgun in his hand as well. Ted's sunglasses flew off, leaving his face showing clear as day. Jack Reddick and Ted looked at each other for a moment. Jack's eyes fixed on Ted's face. He memorized every feature of this man. Every line on his face, every curve, the image of him froze in Jack's mind as clear as day. Jack knew he was looking at the man who'd killed his wife and was probably going to get away. Ted knew he was looking at the husband of the women he'd killed. For almost ten seconds they stared at each other with a mixture of hate and despair.

They aimed at each other. Ted's face was bleeding from the broken glass. He had the advantage; the wind was behind him and he was shooting behind the Car. Jack, on the other hand, was shooting forward into one hundred mile per hour wind. Dirt, wind and small rocks hit Jack's face, so he was unable to get a clear shot at Ted. The police car was dying. Jack shot the gun three times, just hoping to luck out and hit the man.

It didn't work. Ted shot back at Jack and shattered the police car's windshield. Since the windshield was bulletproof, Rosen and Jack were not hurt. Charlie hit the nitrous booster and get up past one hundred twenty miles per hour. Seconds later, the police car's engine locked up. Within a minute, the two cars were far apart. Before Jack knew it, the Cadillac carrying the men who killed his wife was out of sight.

"Goddamn it, where're the State Police? There should be ten squad cars and helicopters by now," Jack asked.

"I didn't call them," Rosen admitted.

"What!"

"I thought this was a no-brainer. Besides, I didn't want those fucking State Police to get credit for this one. I could've made front page for catching the bank robber last year. I could've been promoted and not have to spend all day being shot at," Rosen said about ready to cry.

Jack grabbed the radio, not caring one bit that the State Police stole his glory.

"Call the State Police right now," Jack said to Dispatch.

"I though you said not to, you were gonna handle it yourself?" Dispatch replied.

Jack looked at Rosen, who looked away, ashamed.

"I don't care what Rosen told you! This is Sergeant Jack Reddick, I'm telling you to call them right now!"

"Affirmative."

The police car was dead stopped in the middle of the highway, with smoke coming out of the hood like crazy.

Meanwhile, miles ahead, Ted and Charlie were free as could be. Charlie noticed that the Cadillac was losing power. They exited the Interstate and went to the nearest gas station.

"If we shut off this car, we'll never get it started again," Charlie said.

"Then let's get outta here," Ted replied.

They drove around the area, and happened to find a lake. Ted and Charlie knew what they had to do. They took the scanner and the guns out, then shut off the burning car. Ted and Charlie pushed it with all their strength into the lake. As the Cadillac sank, they heard sizzling noises from the cold water hitting the burning engine.

"Let's get the hell outta here," Charlie said.

"How much money do we have?" Ted asked.

"Three hundred dollars."

"Good; let's go."

"Let's get rid of the shotgun, and keep the .45; it's easier to hide," Charlie said.

"When you bought the shotgun, did they ask to see ID?" Ted asked.

"Who said I bought it? I pawned the wedding ring for the walkietalkies. While the old fart running the place was in the back on the phone, I took the shotgun and ammo."

"Oh, stealing from an old man, huh?"

"Oh, please! He screwed me so bad on the ring, it paid for the gun."

"Yeah," Ted said just to agree.

"I mean it; that ring was worth close to a thousand bucks. He gave me three hundred dollars and walkie-talkies for it. Besides I wore that wedding ring for twenty years, that should mean something."

Ted nodded his head, threw the shotgun and ammo into the lake. The Cadillac he'd owned most of his adult life was so deep in the water all that could be seen were bubbles in the lake. Ted took one more look at his old Cadillac before it was gone forever. He remembered how happy he'd been to get it over twenty years ago. Little did he know then what was going to happen.

He and Charlie walked away from lake, onto a side street, where they called a cab. About the time it showed up, the scanner came on.

"Attention, all State Police: look for a 70's Cadillac. The windows are broken, and it's sustained bullet holes. Suspects are two white males, headed east on the Interstate. They are wanted for two counts of first-degree murder," the scanner said.

Ted and Charlie looked at each other, hoping the cab driver hadn't heard it.

"Where do ya wanna go?" the cab driver asked.

"Take us across the line into Colorado," Ted said.

"Yes, sir."

Chapter 2

Jack Reddick

Jack Reddick was at the hospital, waiting until they took Peggy to the morgue. Officer Marshall was also taken to the morgue. Jack had nothing except a burned image in his head, of the man who had killed his wife. He knew the image of the man would never go away until he was found.

Jack went home, only to be the one to break the horrible news to the kids about their mom. A few minutes after he'd told his eleven-year-old son Andy and his fourteen-year-old daughter Nita what happened, the doorbell rang. The kids were crying uncontrollably as Jack went to the door.

"Sergeant Reddick? I'm Detective Donny; this is my partner Detective Johnson. I believe you know why we're here."

"Of course, come in," Jack said.

Jack could hardly hear Donny, because the kids were crying so loud. As the two six-foot tall, bulldog-faced men in their creased trench coats came in, Jack was still trying to comfort the kids. Nita wiped away the last tear from her glassy, light-blue eyes. Wisely, Jack asked both kids to leave the room before he spoke with the detectives.

"Mr. Reddick, we know you're a cop. I'm sure you know that we must ask you some very ugly questions," Donny said.

"Yes, I know, go for it," Jack replied.

"All right, first, have you arrested anyone who said they would get you back? Any big time arrests at all?"

"I arrest lots of people, but none of them have threatened me."

"Any strange phone calls? People ringing the doorbell and running?" Johnson said.

"Nope."

"Are you sure you can't think of anyone, even from an old case years ago, who would have done this?" Donny asked.

Jack shook his head. "No. When Officer Rosen and I were in pursuit, one of the men stuck his head out the Caddy window. I saw exactly what he looked like. That image will never leave me."

"The man didn't look familiar?" Johnson asked.

"No, I've never seen that man before. I promise you that on the force I never forget a face, even if it's just a speeding ticket. I would've remembered; I can tell you, I've never seen him."

"Was Peggy ever into drugs? Or owed anyone money?' Johnson asked.

"Oh, no, Peggy never did drugs. We never borrowed money from anyone; she never cheated on me or anything."

"Did she ever leave the house for long periods of time?" Donny asked.

"Well, she did just get back from Nebraska a month ago."

"What was she doing out there?"

"Her mother was dying of cancer, and she wanted to be with her."

"How long did she stay out there?"

"Almost five, or maybe six months; when her mother finally died, she came home."

Donny and Johnson took many pages of notes, then looked at each other for a moment.

"Do you think it was someone from Nebraska who did this?" Johnson asked.

Again Jack shook his head. "I really doubt it. Peggy grew up there; everyone knew her. I don't see why taking care of her sick mother could've gotten her into trouble."

"Look, Jack, you're a cop," Donny said. "I think you know this is really bad. I talked to the teacher who saw the man enter the school. From what she told us, these men didn't pick Peggy's name out of a hat. They were looking specifically for her."

Jack put his hands over his face.

"Why couldn't that teacher have stopped him?" Jack asked.

"Come on, Jack, she's seventy-two-years-old and under one hundred pounds. How was she gonna stop a six-foot tall, two hundred pound man with a gun?" Johnson said.

"I know, but it's just a total mystery. Why would someone want to kill Peggy?"

"Jack, once again, we need to make sure you aren't leaving something out. No matter how bad or embarrassing it is, we need to know, if we're ever gonna find these guys," Donny said.

"Nothing else, I swear."

"So all we have was that some guy killed Peggy for no reason at all," Johnson said glumly. "State Police have had no luck finding them, or the Cadillac."

"How could they miss that car?" Jack wondered. "It's huge, and all the windows were shot out."

The Detectives had no answer. They got to their feet.

"Well, you guys try to hang in there. Watch the kids and all that good stuff. We'll call you with any news, okay?" Donny said.

"Yes, thank you, gentlemen." Jack showed them to the door.

That first night was tough. Jack had to comfort the kids and himself. Some friends came over, but it brought little relief. Jack was struggling mightily, because he couldn't get the image of that man out of his head. At least now, if he saw the man again, he would recognize him. Although he figured the police were probably going to throw this case in the good old unsolved files, he was planning an investigation of his own. This time, it was personal.

By the one-year anniversary, Jack still had no clue to who had killed his wife. He was a great father, but it was tough being alone. He socialized with women, but knew he could never marry again. Nita was now fifteen and Andy was twelve. The police had given up on the case, but Jack, on the other hand, was out to find the killers.

"Hey, kids, I have a three day weekend coming up. What do you say we go skiing in Colorado?" Jack said just before Thanksgiving.

Jack and Peggy used to go skiing when they first got married, but they hadn't taken the kids in a while. On the way there, Jack stopped at every rest stop and gas station he could, even if he didn't need gas. He drove around in many of the towns along the way, just to look around. The trip took more than a day because Jack stopped so much.

"Dad, we know what your doing and it's far-fetched," Andy said.

"Well, it's a known fact that the odds of me running into this man again will increase if I'm in more places."

They finally made it to the ski resort. Jack and the kids had fun, but it just wasn't the same without Peggy. The thought that they'd only gone out of town to look around for this man ruined it. Jack had taken many road trips in the past year, just to look around. Over that next year, it seemed the kids never saw him, unless he was on a searching road trip.

By the two-year anniversary of their mother's death, the kids were almost grown up. One day at school, Nita couldn't take it any more. She went to see the school counselor. Before her mother's death, she had always worn clothes that had cartoon figures on them. Now she wore black jeans and black shirts and walked hunched over all the time. Her long golden hair had always been brushed and shining when Peggy was around. Now it was hardly washed, with many split ends.

On the way to the counseling office, Nita saw a flyer for the cheerleading team. All she could do at the thought of cheerleading was cry. Two years ago, she'd have signed up in a heartbeat. Now she knew she couldn't fit in. Two years ago, she'd been slim, with a firm chest and a clean, smooth face. Now her sagging chest and big butt matched her fat stomach; it seemed all she did in her free time was eat. Her pores were clogged, her face dull.

"Cheerleader girls are dumb and giggly, but I have nothing to giggle about," Nita said to her school counselor, Mrs. Kinley.

"I'm sure your father is trying his best," Kinley said.

"Yeah, right! He spent all his free time searching for this man. If God came down to my dad and told him to trade me and my brother in just to find this man, he would do it."

"Oh, that's not true; he probably just needs to know why."

"It's like this man killed my mother and my father. My dad is dead to me. He isn't the man I grew up with; he's a stranger."

"I can refer you to a doctor who can prescribe some antidepressants for you," Mrs. Kinley suggested.

"No way; I don't need them. Drugs are for people who don't know why they're depressed. I know why; I just want to solve the problem, not be drugged up."

"I understand. Who do you think killed your mom?"

"I don't know. I guess we can't blame William Defreno anymore."

"Who is that?"

"Oh, um, my mom was his school counselor when he was in junior high. He caused a bunch of trouble in this town a few years back. I know how he must have felt; wish I could have met him."

"Oh, yes," Mrs. Kinley said. "I do remember reading about him in the newspaper."

"My dad has put over one hundred thousand miles on mom's new car in two years," Nita went on. "He just drove around for hours looking at people, hoping to find this man."

"I don't know what we can do," the counselor said. "I think you need to explain this to your dad."

"He doesn't care, all he cares about is finding this man."

"Well, listen, Nita, if you need anything, my door is open to you."

"Thank you," Nita said as she headed for the door.

A few nights later, Jack was thinking yet again about the man who killed his wife. Whenever the anniversary came, he'd get deep into thought. He would think about what the killers were doing at that same moment. He remembered every detail about what had happened two years ago. The image of the man hanging his head out the window, hadn't faded one bit. Jack fell asleep; instantly he dreamed.

In the dream, he was an old man, thirty years later. The kids were in their late forties, with families of their own. Jack was walking with a cane, and his kids were beside him. They were skiing again in Colorado, but Jack was too old to get on the slopes. He just watched as his kids and grand-kids skied. As they were leaving for the day, they headed to the car in a somewhat good mood. Andy told a joke and all of them started laughing. Jack stopped laughing all of a sudden.

"What's wrong, Dad?" Andy asked.

"Kids, my life has been tough since your mother died. I've moved on, I've taken care of myself and no matter how tempting it was, I never gave up hope in life."

The kids were surprised at Jack's sudden mood change.

"You okay?" Nita asked.

"Yes, I don't know how I made it all these years, but I did. This is why; this exact moment is why I went through thirty years of suffering. Working hard, to bring you kids up right. This is finally my reward, my mission, my reason," Jack said.

The kids were really disturbed. They noticed that when Jack spoke to them, he didn't look at them.

"Daddy, you're scaring me! What is it?" Nita asked.

Jack moved slowly away from them. The kids didn't understand. Jack wouldn't answer them; instead he kept walking forward.

"Dad, tell us now, please. You're not gonna die on us, are you?" Andy asked.

"Nope, everything is gonna be fine," Jack said with a smile.

The kids were still stunned as Jack hugged them.

"It's them, children," Jack said, as he pointed to the two men in front of them. "My mission is complete. I got my wish in life. Those are the men who killed your mom; I finally found them."

Jack and the kids went up to the men. Both the men and Jack looked at each other. It took both of the men a while to realize what was going on. After staring at each other, they both knew. Jack grabbed the main man.

"So, I finally found you, ya wife killing sons of bitches!"

The two men didn't answer. Jack pulled out his gun, aimed it at the man he saw the day of the chase.

"Before I blow your brains out, you're gonna tell me why you did it," Jack said.

"Well, good job, you finally found me. I'm the man you're looking for. Go ahead, shoot me if you think that it's gonna bring back Peggy."

"I know killing you is never gonna bring back Peggy. But at least you'll be gone. But first, why did you do it?"

"Very well, I'll tell you why I did it."

"Hurry up, because the sight of you made me sick. I don't know how long I can resist pulling the trigger on you."

"I did it because Peggy did it."

Suddenly Jack woke up from his dream. It was the middle of the night and sweat rolled off his head. He got up, had a glass of water, and began to think of the dream more. He knew it was just another weird, pointless dream, with no catharsis.

"You did it, because Peggy did it. What does that mean?" Jack said to himself.

He went back to sleep, repeating the phase over and over to himself.

The next day at work, he kept saying the phrase over and over again. No matter how many times he said it, no sense came out of it. Halfway through the day, the Chief of police asked to see Jack in his office.

"What is it chief?" Jack asked.

Chief Mahoney was a dedicated man. Jack always said he looked like a police chief, because he was a huge black guy with a lot of facial hair who wore a light-blue suit to work all the time. With such a unique look to him, he could've easily been in a Police Academy movie. Even though he was big, tough and a police chief, he was quite a nice guy.

"Jack, I've noticed you're really under pressure."

"Yeah."

"Listen, you've been slacking off. I could scold you for it, but instead I'm going to recommend you take the next week off. Maybe go on a road trip, or do something to clear your head."

"I'm sorry, chief, it's just I need to know who killed my wife."

"Well, we can't have you using all your time on one case."

"You don't understand what this has done to me. I can't sleep, I can't eat, and my own children think I'm crazy."

"Like I said, maybe a week off will help you. Don't go looking around weird towns for them. In fact, don't even think of these guys at all."

"I'm not sure I'm doing the right thing. Peggy would've wanted me to raise the kids' right. Then again, I'm sure she'd want me to find out who killed her."

"You know, have you ever heard the phrase 'If you stop looking for something, you will find it'?"

"Yeah, but I can't stop; I dream of this almost once a week. Not one moment has gone by where I haven't thought of the image that I have of this man."

"Jack, maybe we can luck out and they both committed suicide after the shooting. They may be dead already, and this could be a waste of time."

"I actually hope not, 'cause then I'd never know why he did it. I want the law to be the one to kill him. I want his life to be taken against his will, just like Peggy's was. I want him to see what it is like to be killed by someone else."

"Jack, I already told you that you could be in a lot of trouble for your slacking. I'm offering you this because I know what you are going through."

"Thank you; I will take a week off."

"Great; you can leave today. Why don't you go visit your relatives or something? Maybe they'll make you feel better."

"I will. That sounds really good, thanks."

"Bye," Mahoney said.

"Wait one thing!" Jack called out from the doorway.

"What?"

"If you were interrogating a murder suspect, and he told you the reason he said he did it, was because the victim 'did it,' what would you say?"

"Hmm. I'd say that would mean that they did something to them. What that something is, I don't know."

"I don't know, either; I wish I did."

"Have a fun trip; come back refreshed and ready to work. Remember, don't even think about it."

Jack went home and waited for the kids to come home from

school.

"Kids, I have the next week off. I was thinking we should go on a road trip. Where should we go?"

"I don't know," Andy said.

"Why don't we go visit your mother's relatives in Nebraska?" Jack said.

"Okay, it's been almost six years since we all went to Nebraska," Nita said.

Jack called up Peggy's sister Laura in Omaha.

"Oh, um, hi, Jack; I can't believe it's you."

"We'd like to visit you. I'm sure you must be sad since Peggy was killed."

"Oh, you have no idea," Laura said sadly.

She was extremely nervous talking. Jack could hear her fidgeting over the phone. She agreed to let them all stay at her house. Once again, Jack felt sad, going to stay with Laura for the first time without Peggy. It seemed too weird for him, but he figured that Laura needed support just as much as he did. All of them packed quickly and hit the road.

Jack didn't stop to search towns for the murderer along the way. He knew the kids thought it was pointless. Jack didn't want this trip to be another murder case trip. This time, it was his first real vacation, and he was going to enjoy it like a real person, as the chief said to.

Chapter 3

The New Lead

Stopping only for gas, Jack didn't totally forget to look at everyone he saw. When they arrived at Laura's house the next day, she wasn't home.

"I wonder where she is?" Jack said.

"Well, Dad, what do you want to do while we're waiting?" Andy asked.

"Hmm, you know we never did go to your grandma's funeral. I guess we could go visit her grave while we're here."

All three of them got back into the car to go to the cemetery. There were over five thousand graves, so they ask at the office for a map. The cemetery's custodian gave them direction to Peggy's mother's grave. On the way, they passed by many tombstones. Just the sight of the cemetery reminded them all of Peggy. Although the three of them didn't speak to each other at first, they were all thinking the same thing.

Many of the graves had flowers, and signs that said "Mom" or "Dad" on them. Jack looked at one of the graves along the way. The inscription said: "Sleep now, for the Lord holds thee." Another inscription read: "Rest in peace. Our love never died." Jack felt just terrible; he knew Peggy was never coming back, yet so much was still unanswered.

My poor Peggy is dead, while the men who did it are still around! Jack thought.

He didn't share that thought with the kids. He'd promised not to make this another searching-for-the-murderers vacation. Also, he didn't want to sadden them more. He knew they were young and not as tough as he was about this whole thing. Jack had noticed a huge change in both Andy and Nita over the last two years.

Neither of the kids even had a girlfriend or boyfriend. They didn't get involved in sports or anything. Jack knew lately it hadn't matter to him. "Too bad if the kids don't like it, I'm going to find theses guys!" was his attitude. He'd promised himself he would stop looking, but he knew he could never keep that promise. When they arrived at the tombstone, it was as clean as could be.

"Hi, Grandma. Sorry we never came to visit you," Andy said.

"Yeah, I'm glad your mom took care of her before she died," Jack said.

"Yeah, mom and grandma are together again, but I wish they were here," Nita said.

Jack patted the tombstone and smiled. Then something caught his eye.

"Wait a minute. It says June 1997. What the hell? She died in 1999."

The kids looked as well; they all assume it's a misprint.

"Can you believe it? You pay all this money for funerals and they can't even put the right date on here. Come on, lets go give 'em hell," Jack said.

All three of them headed towards the cemetery office. When they got there, Jack asked to see the manager.

"You put the wrong date on this tombstone," Jack said. "This women died in 1999."

The manager looked up the death certificate.

"Nope, here's her death certificate, and it says 1997."

Jack looked at it with shocked eyes, his mouth open.

"It's wrong; she died in 1999. My wife was out here taking care of her for six months. There's no question; it's wrong."

"Sir, I swear it's correct. We have not buried anyone in that part of the cemetery since 1997, and her death certificate is right here."

Jack said nothing more. He and the kids walked out slowly.

"Jesus Christ, if Grandma was already dead in 1999, what was you mother doing out here for six months?" Jack said.

"But why would Mom lie? There's got to be something they're not telling us," Andy said.

At first Jack was mad, but then he became anxious; he might've just stumbled across another lead. As they were driving back to Laura's house, he remembered all the telephone calls and letters from Peggy when she was supposedly helping her dying mother. He didn't get too excited about it, he just figured it was all explainable. Since he was a cop and a detective, he knew this was no little thing. This could shine some light on the so-called motiveless murder of his wife. When they got back to Laura's house, she was home.

"Hey, guys and girls, come on in," she said.

Jack approached her with a little smile on his face. He could see she was freaked out over his little smile.

"What's wrong?" she asked Jack after the kids had gone up to the guest room to put their suitcases away.

"Listen, I won't play games, I want answers and will do whatever it took to get them."

"What do you mean?"

"Look, I don't care if we have to stay at a hotel tonight, I must know about Peggy."

"What?"

"What was she doing out here for six months in 1999?"

"Staying with mom, before she died," she replied nervously.

"Oh, really? It sure was funny your mother had been dead for two years in 1999. What did Peggy do, sleep at the cemetery for six months?"

Laura started to shake and her face went pale. Jack was getting excited now; he knew when somebody acted like this, it meant they were hiding something.

"Please just let it be," she said in a shaky voice.

"Let it be! Are you nuts? Peggy's dead, the men who killed her were out there free as birds. You could provide answers about who they are, and you won't tell me."

Laura began to cry. Real tears came from her green eyes.

"Jack, Peggy would rather her murderers were free than have me tell you what happened," she said while she wiped away the tears.

Jack put his hands on her shoulders violently. Her body locked up instantly.

"Listen! Tell me now. You're gonna hang higher than Billy the Kid if you don't talk."

Laura cried harder, trembling from Jack yelling at her. At that moment Jack forgot he was talking to Peggy's sister. In his mind, he was interrogating a suspect. After ten seconds he came back to reality, realizing how stupid he sounded mentioning Billy the Kid.

"I don't know if it would be good for you to know," Laura said.

"Oh I get it! Peggy was cheating on me. The man she was with was the killer, and he probably lives here in town, huh?"

"No, I wish it were that easy. This was much more complicated than a simple affair."

"Really?" Jack pondered.

"Yes, Peggy would never cheat on you. She would never want her family to be brought down by something she did so many years ago."

Jack calmed down and he and Laura sat down.

"I don't understand," Jack said.

"Peggy loved you all very much; she would do anything to protect you and the kids. Even if it meant lying."

"Spill your guts; I gotta know all."

"Well, you know that Peggy had a double counseling and pharmacy degree, right?"

"Yes."

"And you remember that when the kids were small she worked as a court-appointed counselor?" Jack nodded.

"What you didn't know was that before you two were married, since her job was mandated by the court, she could prescribe anything, and these people would have to pay it. Peggy was a hard-core believer for women's rights and a feminist. She loved to help women get back at their domineering husbands. One time she was sued for bad advice. A client of hers broke her probation and killed her husband. The women claimed it was Peggy's counseling that pushed her over the edge."

Jack sat in the old country style sofa hoping at any moment

Laura would say who the murderers were.

"Peggy had no malpractice insurance, so she just kept asking for delays before going to court. While she was supposedly having migraine headaches in 1994, she was really going to trials, not doctors. In 1996 she was ordered to pay $65,000 in restitution. You guys were struggling enough with money, so she didn't pay it. Well, then in late 1998, she got news that they could take away the house if she didn't pay it by the summer of 1999. Peggy didn't want you guys to lose your home and she hated sneaking around."

"I see now, thinking back, there were times she would always get up early to grab the mail and dive for the telephone," Jack said.

"Yep."

"So, how did she come up with the money? I never heard a thing about it, and we never did lose the house."

Laura wiped away another tear.

"Are you sure you are ready for this?" she asked as Andy and Nita crept downstairs, concerned at the adults' ominous tone. "Maybe the kids should leave the room."

"No, they can stay here; we're in this together. We know Peggy was just trying to help us, and whatever she did to get the money was for good."

"I'm glad you can handle it."

"Was it drugs?"

"No, well, not illegal drugs like cocaine. Instead over-the-counter drugs and lots of cunning counseling."

" Counseling?" Jack echoed. He sighed. "Okay, let's hear it all."

"Well, she still needed $53,000 by 1998. The only thing she had to make money was that she was a certified counselor and pharmacist. She heard that there was a real need for marriage counselors in Detroit. Also, office space was cheap, so she set up a marriage counseling shop out there for six months. Having her own degree for medication as well as professional counseling made her even more money than she needed, in just six months. Peggy was always for women's rights. In fact, that's how she got into this trouble, because of her advice. Peggy said that she helped many women divorce bad husbands. But she also charged a lot of money for her services, and prescribed a lot of medication, sometimes more than was needed, and some of it was addicting. So she sort of created a market for her services. She did it all legally, and helped many women get free of their husbands, although I suspect she broke up a lot of good homes as well."

"So, Peggy was a professional home wrecker, huh?" Jack said.

"Well, I don't think she saw it that way."

"Okay, so who killed her? I have this image in my head, it follows me around all day and night. I see his face everywhere I go, who is he?

"I don't know."

"Do you have addresses of where her office was? Where she stayed? Anything at all?"

"Yes, I will give them to you. I even have the address for the local TV station her commercials were on."

"Commercials?"

Jack was breathing heavily and he felt a baseball bat couldn't have hit him as hard as the truth about his ultra-feminist wife.

"So, why didn't you tell me this when she was killed?" Jack asked. "The killers could've been caught by now."

"I honestly don't think the killer came from Detroit. Peggy didn't use her real name, and she left no evidence of who she was or where she went. All records of her real name and identity were protected and sealed. The post office couldn't give out her forwarding address. There was no way anyone could have found out about her."

"What was her so-called name?" Jack asked.

"Ann Ritz."

Jack and the kids looked at each other and couldn't believe it.

"I'm still gonna check it out. I've had no luck in two years finding leads that the men are from where we live," Jack said.

"I'm so sorry, but Peggy only did it because she loved you. I only lied because I loved her."

"I can't believe she was such a bitch; she acted like the wonderful little suburban daisy wife. She cooked and cleaned and wore cute little aprons."

"Yes, she loved her kids, but she was an ultra feminist. She was in the parade for women's rights several times. She loved to get other women to fight back at their husbands."

"She never bossed me around," Jack protested.

"She said you were the perfect husband; she shaped you right, and took care of you."

"I did wonder why she all of a sudden bought a new car, without even having payments. Oh yeah, she even bought the kids all new toys and clothes when she came home in 1999."

"Yep, she made lots of money off the women of Detroit. She even bought the car in Detroit under the name Ann Ritz. She had to sell the car to herself so she could change the title to Peggy Reddick."

"Hmm, I see what you mean; she covered her bases well. It would be almost impossible for someone to find her. If she could con her own family for so many years, she must have been good enough to not leave a paper trail of where she was."

Laura cried more.

"I'm sorry I had to yell," Jack said as he hugged Laura.

"So what now?" she asked.

"Tomorrow I'm gonna head to Detroit to get leads."

"Great," she said. "The kids can stay here till you get back."

Jack smiled. He knew the truth about Peggy. It didn't mean much; he still had no idea to who the man was whose image was stuck in his head. Could he possible be from Detroit? Or would this only complicate a case that was already impossible to solve? Jack took sleeping pills that night so he could keep his mind off the case. Even though he'd promised himself and the kids this was just going to be a vacation, this was the first new lead he had had in years.

At 7:00 A.M. Jack woke up, grabbed some coffee, and was on his way to Detroit. He didn't stop except for gasoline. When he arrived, the big city overwhelmed him. After nearly an hour of driving around and asking for directions, he finally found the office his wife had worked out of. It was an insurance office now. He realized just staring at the office building would get him nowhere. As he stood in front of the building, he could almost see his wife coming out the door. Jack realized that the killers might have lived around here. He made his way to the TV station. After forty minutes of research, the staff was able to find the commercial for Ann Ritz. Even with her hair curled and parted in the middle, it didn't take more than a second to see that it was his wife.

"I wonder what I was doing at the exact moment she filmed this?" Jack said to himself.

He looked at the tape for a while. It didn't suggest any leads. Almost three years had gone by since Peggy was here. Because it was such a huge city, probably nobody would remember her. Jack wandered the big city all day.

"Peggy, I forgive you for what you did, and for lying. But I gotta know who killed you, and I bet you know who it is," Jack said out loud.

He stayed at a hotel called The Detroit Inn, in Room 123. He noticed a dead rat behind the toilet. He felt bizarre staying at this hotel, especially in Room 123, but didn't know why. There was just something creepy about this room that made his body shake from time to time.

The next morning he headed back to Nebraska to get the kids. When he got to Laura's house, they were all waiting for him.

"What did you find?" Andy asked.

"Well, just that your mother was a marriage counselor, and that she's still dead."

Laura and the kids were disappointed. All four of them knew the new lead didn't really mean much, but someday it could. The next morning Jack and the kids headed for home. They were gloomy because the vacation had turned out to be just another searching road trip. On the good side, it had given Jack the biggest lead in years. When he got back to work he wasn't as refreshed as the chief had hoped he would be. He tried his best to do the job and not anger anyone.

Chapter 4

Junkyard Anger

In early 2002, two men walked into a repair shop and junkyard in north Oklahoma.

"Can I help you?" the clerk asked.

The clerk, whose name was Eddie, was a true junkyard man. He was about 5' 8", fat, hairy, and wore dirty suspenders. He glared at the two men as he talked to them.

"Yes, you remember me?" the first man asked. "You fixed the transmission for my Cadillac, three months ago."

"Oh, yeah, so what do you want now?" Eddie said in a rude tone.

"Well, this goddamn thing doesn't work," the first man said as he put the transmission on the counter.

"Listen, buddy, I told ya when I fixed it that this was a weird transmission. I don't know where you got it, but it isn't a standard GM Tranny."

"Look, Eddie, I paid you five hundred dollars to fix it and explained that it was a special tranny. You said you could fix it, and you didn't."

"Well don't fuckin' blame me; we did the best we could," Eddie growled.

Another big fat hairy clerk named Bud came out of the back room. Eddie and Bud looked like twins, except Bud was taller, and had both of his front teeth.

"What's wrong?" Bud said in a deep voice.

"I just want a refund, and everything will be fine," the first man said.

"That's all we want," the second man said.

"No mother fuckin' refunds," Bud replied. "Can't you read?"

"What kind of junkyard is this? You can't even fix a simple transmission?" the first man asked.

"I done told you, it's not a standard tranny. Hell, man, I fixed the tranny on my Camaro sitting out front; it never once gave me problems. This tranny you have is too high performance or whatever to be fixed. It was fuckin' rusted out. Where the hell'd you get it -- the bottom of a lake?"

"Oh, that yellow Camaro is yours, huh?" the first man said.

"Yep, she's my pride and joy," Eddie replied.

"So, why is it we can't have the five hundred dollars back?" the second man wanted to know.

"Are you fuckin' deaf and stupid? No fuckin' refunds!" Bud yelled.

The two men were getting mad at Bud and Eddie for yelling and waving their arms at them.

"Okay, last chance," the first man said. "May I please have a refund, or even a store credit for other parts?"

"Get the fuck outta here!!" Eddie said.

The two men looked at each other and smiled.

"Okay, fine, but you might wanna watch outside," the first man said.

Eddie and Bud watched the two men. First they saw them put the broken transmission in the trunk of the Cadillac they'd driven up in. The first man pulled a baseball bat out of the trunk. The second man got into the Cadillac and started it up. The first man walked toward Eddie's yellow Camaro.

"Hey, fuckers!" he yelled. "If I can't have the five hundred dollars, neither can you!"

The man smashed the windshield and the driver's window of Eddie's Camaro. The sounded of shattering glass could be heard throughout the whole junkyard. The man's crazy laughter could be heard even more, as he violently smashed the hell out of Eddie's nice, clean Camaro.

"Mother-fuckers!" Bud yelled.

Eddie grabbed a baseball bat and Bud grabbed a BB gun they kept under the counter. They ran outside, and Eddie shut the gates so the two men were trapped inside the yard. The steel gates were strong enough that even the Cadillac couldn't drive through them.

"Okay, if that's the way you wanna play. I'm gonna put you in the fuckin' ground for wrecking my Camaro," Eddie said.

Bud aimed the BB gun at the two men. Eddie approached the first man and was ready to hit him with the bat. Suddenly, before Eddie could get close enough to them, the first man pulled out a .45 handgun and aimed it right at Eddie's face. Eddie dropped the bat and backed away.

"Open the gates now, boys," the first man said.

"Fuck you," Eddie replied.

"Oh, so you think I'm fucking around here? You think the BB gun that your little girlfriend Bud over there is holding is gonna save you?"

The man cocked the gun. Both Eddie and Bud could see he was ready the pull that trigger at any moment. Bud put down the BB gun and put his hands up. Eddie was feeling cockier than Bud.

"You won't shoot me, and you ain't leaving until we can decide how much you owe me for busting up my car," Eddie said.

"Oh, don't think I'll do it, huh? Well, I got news for you. I've already killed two people. One of them was a cop. Since they can only hang me once, I outta plug you and your ass-buddy over there full of holes. Now open the gate."

Even Eddie was getting a little scared, because the man sounded so serious when he said he'd killed two people.

"Jesus Christ, Eddie! Open the gates!" Bud stuttered.

Eddie nodded his head, but he was angry as hell. He opened the gate and the men got into the Cadillac.

"I better never see your asses around here again!" Eddie said.

The first man rolled down the window.

"Oh, don't worry; you won't," he said.

Both of them drove off slowly at first, but then sped up. Eddie was red-hot and headed towards the junkyard tow truck.

"I'm gonna kill those mother-fuckers!" he said.

Although inside Eddie was scared speechless, he acted like he wasn't to look tough in front of Bud.

"Fuck 'em! I ain't getting shot by no .45 handgun. We gotta call the sheriff," Bud said.

"Goddamn it! Look at my car."

They both looked at it for a moment. The windshield, the driver's window, the back window and the hood were all smashed. Both of them ran inside to call the sheriff. After ten minutes, he arrived. They could see the sunlight reflecting off his badge. The sheriff was so tall and muscular, Eddie looked like a little boy next to him. Bud could see his reflection, clear as day, in the sheriff's silver mirrored sunglasses. Eddie got the sheriff a Coke, because his tanned, wrinkled, sweaty face looked hot as he took out a notepad and a pencil.

"Hello, I'm Sheriff Terry, can y'all tell me what they all look like?"

"They were both white, um, tall, short hair, maybe forty, and drove an old Cadillac," Eddie replied.

"That's all ya know? They let slip any names or say anything unusual?"

"Well, the transmission they brought in was something we've never seen before. I'm not sure where they got such a high performance transmission for a Cadillac."

"Is that how this started?"

"Yep, they asked us to fix this transmission. I told him I would give it my best, but couldn't guarantee anything. Then they come back and want a refund, after I already told them I couldn't guarantee anything."

"Well, was that all that set them off?"

"Pretty much. I was real polite, and I explained the situation and then all of a sudden here he came with this baseball bat to my car," Eddie said.

"Didn't ya say on the telephone that ya had them trapped in here with the gates shut?"

"Yeah, but they put a .45 handgun to my face, so I opened the gates and out they went."

"Did they say where they were headed? Or do ya know?"

"No, but I would guess there are headed for Kansas or Texas."

The sheriff wrote down everything Eddie said.

"Oh, and one more thing," Bud interrupted.

"What might that be?" Sheriff Terry said.

"When he had the .45 aimed at Eddie, he said that he had already killed two people and that one of them was a cop."

"Hmm, ya know, he was probably just trying to intimidate ya all with big words."

"Honestly, I don't think so. I'm no cop, but I can tell you, just by the man's voice and the way his finger was ready to pull the trigger, that he might not be kiddin' around," Bud said.

"Do ya really think so?"

"Yes, if you had just heard the seriousness of his voice. He even made the comment that 'they could only hang him once.'"

Sheriff Terry thought about it for a moment.

"This may sound stupid, but did he happen to mention where and when he killed these folks?"

Eddie laughed, and Bud hit him on the back of the head with his hand.

"No, we opened the gates before we got into a deep conversation with these psychos," Bud said.

"Sounded kinda serious, so I'm gonna be putting out a national APB."

"What's that?" Eddie asked.

"It means; all points bulletin. It's a national bulletin that all police departments in the country will receive. It will tell them to look up any recent or old murder cases. If there are any that involved two people getting murdered with a .45 handgun, one being a cop, and the killers match your description, then we can get the feds involved."

"Wow, that would be great," Bud replied.

"Honestly, though, ya have to realize that if they really are wanted for murder, they would probably not even get arrested for what they did to your car, and there will be no restitution."

Bud and Eddie nodded their heads.

"That's all right. Even if we can't get money out of them, I'll personally be there, when they fry those bastards," Bud said.

"I'll keep y'all informed. Right now I wanna get back to the station and call the State Police."

"Great, thanks," Bud replied.

"Yep. Who knew? Maybe we can get 'em before they cross the state line."

Sheriff Terry left, Eddie and Bud went back inside, both cursing up a storm about the car. A national APB about the case was put out within two days. The APB reached the small city in Utah where Jack Reddick worked.

It was a normal morning for Jack; bags under the eyes, and his hair a mess. The typical morning started by drinking lots of coffee. He breezed through the APB lists. There were many of them from different states. Ready to walk away to get more coffee, he decided to look over them again. It caught his eye about two men killing a cop and another person with a .45 handgun. Jack read the descriptions again.

"I'm telling you, these might be the men who killed my wife and that cop where I live," Jack said to Chief Mahoney.

"Maybe, but don't put all your hope in it," Chief Mahoney said.

"Hell, no, but I'd like to go to Oklahoma and talk to the junkyard men personally."

"I can grant permission for that. You must realize that they'll not be required to talk to you since we're in a different state. Also you'll have to use your own car. The police department will compensate you for time and gas."

"They'll talk to me, I don't see why they wouldn't wanna help me find these guys. I'm sure they want them as much as I do."

"Well like I said, you can go, but don't try to act like they're required to talk to you, we could get sued, everything must be voluntary."

"I won't bully them, I'd like to get going, like, right now so the descriptions are still fresh to these guys."

"All right, just fill out this paperwork, so you get paid, and you can head on your way."

"Thank you chief; I don't know what I would do without you."

"You're welcome, and to be honest, I really wanna help you. Also any case where a wife and a cop are murdered, is top priority to me."

Once again, Jack had to say goodbye to the kids so he could go on a road trip to Oklahoma. The kids didn't even care. On the long boring drive, he thought of what he was going to say to these guys, so they would give accurate descriptions. When Jack reached the Oklahoma state line, he decided to look around a bit. Every time he saw an old Cadillac he'd examine the driver. None of the Cadillacs he saw contained the man he was looking for.

He arrived at the junkyard and could see the Camaro that was destroyed. Looking at it, he realized he could be standing at the same place, where the man he had put every moment of the last three years into might have been. Jack stood there waiting for Bud and Eddie. It gave him great disgruntlement to think that those men had been trapped in behind the gates.

"Oh, God, if only I could have been here!" Jack said to himself.

Jack knew if he had been here, he would have taken a chance and had a shoot-out with the man, rather than let him go. The internal struggle made him pace around and talk to himself like a crazy person. Bud and Eddie looked outside at Jack talking to himself.

"Oh, great, we got another nutcase on our hands," Eddie said to Bud.

"What do you want?" Eddie said to Jack.

"Are you Eddie and Bud?" Jack asked.

"Yep."

"Well, I'm a private eye who's trying to solve a murder."

"Oh really? Look, we're pretty busy," Bud replied.

"Yes, well, it's very possible that the men who destroyed your nice car might be they guys we're looking for. I want to talk to you guys. I brought some suds; we can drink while we're talking," Jack said as he handed Bud and Eddie a six-pack of Budweiser.

Bud and Eddie got excited and less skeptical of the man talking to himself.

"Sure, let's chat, buddy boy," Bud said.

"Thanks," Jack said, relieved that the men were willing to help.

"I don't know if there's anything we didn't say to the sheriff," Bud said.

"I know, I got the descriptions of the men from the APB. I was wondering about this Cadillac they were driving."

"It was a 1978 Coupe DeVille, and it looked pretty shabby," Eddie said.

"Yes, but I bet it was fast with that weird transmission in it," Bud interrupted.

"Hmm, you know they used an old Cadillac to commit the murders," Jack said.

"Oh, really? Nobody told us anything," Eddie replied, taking a swig of beer.

"Yeah, we never even knew they killed someone. We thought they were fuckin' with us," Bud added as he threw the first empty can on the ground and opened another.

"Was this Cadillac really beat up? Or maybe in really good shape in some areas from being fixed up?"

"It was rough, but nothing less than twenty-three years of normal wear and tear," Bud said.

"What was so weird about the transmission?"

"It wasn't a standard tranny; he must have either spent thousands to have it custom made, or he was a really good engineer. GM never released a high performance transmission like this one," Bud replied.

"Burrrp!" Eddie said as he dropped his first empty can on the ground and opened another. Jack grabbed a beer for himself so he would fit in. He noticed there was only one left, after only fifteen minutes of talking.

"What else can you tell us about this guy? And the murder case; maybe we can help more," Eddie said.

"Well, if he is the guy I'm looking for, he is either from Utah, Nebraska, or even Detroit."

Bud and Eddie were trying to think if there was anything about the two men that could be traced to any of those three places.

"Come to think of it, he didn't have much of a Southern accent, or even a Midwest; he sounded like a city boy," Bud said.

"Really," Jack replied.

"So let me get this right, he used another old Caddy to commit the murders with," Eddie said.

"Yep," Jack replied.

Bud laughed and took a swig of a beer.

"This guy sure likes Cadillacs," Bud said.

"Yeah, I'll bet he would be in heaven living in Detroit; ain't that where the GM plant is?" Eddie said.

The two clerks were just rambling like junkyard drunks. They didn't realize they might have helped the case big time.

"Holy shit!" Jack said suddenly.

"What is it?" Bud asked.

"You said the transmission was definitely not available to the public, right?" Jack said.

"No way; it was custom engineered," Bud said.

Jack's eyes got bright as he smiled.

"Fuckin' son of a bitch, I'll bet he worked for the GM plant in Detroit!" Jack said.

"That would sure explain a lot, especially the weird transmission. Now, come to think of it, the two of 'em knew a hell of a lot about GM cars," Bud said.

"Thank you so much! I will, well, you know, call you if I get some information on this," Jack said excitedly.

"You're welcome," Bud said.

Jack looked around for a trashcan for his half-empty can. Bud took it out of his hand, gulped down what was left, then dropped it on the ground with the other five empty cans.

"Thanks. Sorry about your car," Jack said as he got into his own car and drove off.

Jack drove off so fast, he didn't even hear Bud's response to the sympathy note he gave towards Eddie's lost Camaro. He was laughing as he got back onto the highway.

Two hundred miles towards Detroit, the car started acting up. Jack pulled into a gas station with the engine smoking. Even though the car was only three years old, Jack and Peggy had both put a lot of miles on it. After Jack let it cool and added oil, it was ready to go again. After fourteen boring hours total, he made it back to Detroit. He found the GM plant was as big as a small city. Jack knew it might be tough to find out if the man he needed had worked here. He had to ask six different people before he got to the records office. Jack approached the records clerk and flashed his polished police badge.

"I need information on an employee who worked here in early 1999," Jack said, not even caring if he sounded like he was bullying.

"For what department?" the girl asked.

"He was with Cadillac, I believe."

The girl typed something on her computer.

"Okay, we hired over sixty-five employees just for Cadillac in 1999," she said.

"Well, how about employees who were fired or quit?"

"Oh, God, we can't keep track of all the employees we fire. We have a really high turnover rate."

"Really? You don't keep applications?"

"Only for a year; the only way they'd be in our computer is if they were here at least ten years."

She picked up her phone. "Benny Stone, could you come down to records please?" she said into the phone.

"Benny is the man in charge of Cadillac," she said to Jack.

While they were waiting, Jack was thinking of what to say. There were so many possibilities. Maybe his suspect had quit; maybe he was fired or quit before 1999. Maybe he still worked here; maybe he'd just stolen the transmission from a friend who worked here. Maybe he'd never worked here at all and this was yet another dead lead. Just then Benny walked in.

"This man is looking for someone who was fired or quit in 1999," the girl said to Benny.

"Well, maybe. I just don't know for sure," Jack said.

Benny got on the computer and looked up his own records.

"Well, there were a few that I have had to fire. If they only worked here a few months, I don't even bother to record it," Benny said.

"Can I look?" Jack asked.

"Well, I guess."

Jack looked at the records of thirteen employees who had worked for Cadillac for more than ten years before being fired.

"Oh, wait, that was the year I had to fire the head sales manager," Benny said.

Jack was busy studying the names and wasn't paying much attention.

"Oh, yeah? Who was that?" he asked vaguely.

"Hmm, Theodore...or Teddy, as his friends called him."

"Ted who?"

"Um, I think it was Ted Amichi; yeah, that's what it was."

"Theodore Amichi, huh?" Jack replied as he copied the thirteen names.

"Yep, he was here over twenty years, and made it all the way to sales manager."

"Wow, twenty years; that has got to suck to get fired after all that time," Jack said hoping Benny wouldn't ask him to leave.

"I didn't want to do it; he was a great worker. He just couldn't handle the job after his wife divorced him."

Jack stopped looking at the names and paid attention to Benny.

"Did you say his wife divorced him?"

"Yep. I even remember the day when the sheriff served him his divorce papers at work."

"Do you have a picture of Teddy?"

"Yes, but it was taken in 1999 for his security card; I have no recent pictures of him."

"That's what I want. Can I see it?"

"Okay give me a minute!"

Benny was annoyed at Jack's attitude. Jack was glad the photo was from 1999, because that was the last time he'd seen the man.

"Here it is," Benny said.

Jack looked at the picture. It was clear now. The image of the man aiming a gun out of the car at him, was still burned in his head. Also, the image of his wife bleeding to death was coming up, too. He pictured Peggy smiling for once, instead of the usual image of her face smashed as she was rushed to the hospital. Jack stared at the picture for over two minutes. He had finally found out who the man was who had killed his wife.

"Do you know where Teddy is?" Jack asked quietly.

"Oh, I haven't seen him in years, though I do know his best friend was Charlie Fletcher," Benny said.

"Can I copy some of their information?"

"Well, I've already said too much," Benny said.

Jack reached for his handcuffs. Even though he couldn't do anything to Benny, it scared him.

"Sure, I can tell you anything," Benny said, changing his mind in a hurry. "I even know Ted and Charlie's birthdays and their middle names."

Jack copied what was needed from the computer records.

"Thank you," he said tightly.

He knew it wasn't over yet, but he was closer. He knew the gunman's name, the driver's name, and that the last place they'd been was Oklahoma. Jack felt that all the years of endless driving through cities and wandering might finally be paying off.

"I found him, chief; it's him. His name is Theodore Amichi and his partner is Charlie Fletcher. Put out a warrant for questioning for them on NCIC," Jack said on his cell phone, driving home.

"Good job, Jackie; you'll make sergeant for this."

"I'm already sergeant."

"Oh, yeah, I forgot. Anyway, do you think they are still using their real names?"

"Probably, since they think nobody knew who they are."

"Great, well, I should see you here in a few days then, huh?"

"Yes, but I might check telephone books along the way. There's a slight chance he might be listed, since they don't even know they are wanted."

"Whatever; 'bye now," Chief Mahoney said.

Chapter 5

The Wrong Turn

Before leaving the city, he looked in the Michigan white pages for Charlie and Ted. A few listings for each name came up. Jack was tired, and realized he would be better off letting the FBI and NCIC get them. Looking at one of the Ted Amichi listings, he saw it has the same letter in the middle name as his Ted. Jack reminded himself that Ted probably wasn't here but, fixated on this case, he got in his car, drove to the house in the listing. Jack grabbed his briefcase, to look like a salesman. He went up to the house, knocked on the door.

"Are you Ted Amichi?"

"Yeah, what do ya want?" Ted said.

This Ted was about 5'5", three hundred pounds, with his belly hanging out of his torn, dirty tank top. The first thing Jack noticed was the shabby beard, and the horrible smell.

"Sir, I'd like to offer you health insurance at a price you can't miss out on," Jack said.

"Get the hell off my property, now!"

"Yes sir," Jack said.

As Jack left, he wondered what he would've done if this fat derelict had actually said he wanted the insurance. He felt a bit ashamed of himself for wasting so much time, when he knew it couldn't have been the right Ted.

Jack hit the highway, once again promising himself to go straight home. Once again, he lied to himself, taking the turnoff to Oklahoma, to the town where the junkyard was. He didn't want to waste more of the junkyard guys' time, so he combed the city again.

40

Every time the cellular phone rang he'd jump, hoping it was the news that the men had been caught. Deep inside he knew it would take a while for Ted to be found.

Jack stopped at a gas station ten miles from the Kansas border. The car was overheating again, so he went for a walk, while it cooled. A block away, at another gas station, he saw two guys cleaning out their old Cadillac. Jack ran over to them. One man was six feet tall, heavy, wearing a hat and sunglasses. Could it be them? Could this be it? Jack thought. He saw them start the car. It looked like they were going to drive away. Being on foot, he knew he couldn't catch them, if they drove away. The man he thought was the shooter, was throwing one last empty quart of oil in the trash. The man still had his hat and sunglasses on when Jack got up behind him.

"Gotcha!" Jack yelled as he threw the man against the car.

"What the hell?" the man yelled.

"You killed my wife, now put your hands behind your back!"

"What are you talking about? You crazy old fool."

"Shut up, Ted," Jack said as he put cuffs on him.

The other man came up to them to see what was going on.

"Oh, and as for you, Charlie, you're under arrest, too," Jack said.

"Who the hell do you think you are?" the other man said.

Jack flashed his police badge. The men didn't see its State of Utah logo.

"We didn't do anything," the other man said.

Jack threw the first handcuffed man on the ground. After a bit of shoving and pushing, Jack had the second man in cuffs as well. Three officers from the city police showed up.

"What are you doin'?" The officer asked in a hick tone of voice.

"These two men are wanted in Utah for murder," Jack replied.

"Fuck you, we are not, you crackhead!" the first man said.

The first man's glasses and hat fell off. Jack looked at him for the second time, only to be horrified to see he didn't really look like Ted. Maybe age had changed his appearance.

"Who are you?" the cop asked Jack.

"I'm Jack Reddick; I'm a Sergeant and Detective from Utah. These men are Ted Amichi and Charlie Fletcher."

The officers reached into the two men's pockets, got out their wallets. According to their licenses, they were not Ted Amichi or Charlie Fletcher.

"Mr. Reddick, you cannot just beat up and arrest two men you think are murderers. Especially since you have no jurisdiction in this state," the officer said.

"But they're wanted men," Jack replied.

"Not according to their licenses."

"Well, they could be fake."

The three officers went to their cars and talked. They looked in NCIC to see that Ted and Charlie were wanted. A further test would be needed, to prove if these two men were them. The cops got back out of the car.

"Mr. Reddick, put your hands behind your back," one cop said.

"What! Why?" Jack demanded.

"You might be under arrest for assault."

"What do you mean 'might'?"

"Here's the deal...if these men are Ted and Charlie, you'll be released, and they will be sent to Utah. If they're not, you'll be under arrest for assault."

Jack was shaking, because the more he looked at the man, the more doubt he had that it was Ted Amichi.

The cop frisked Jack so hard it ripped his coat.

"Oh, what do we have here?" the cop said as he pulled out Jack's handgun.

"Why would you be carrying this?" the second cop asked.

"I told you, I'm a cop."

"Oh, yeah, one of them big city cops; we know all about you guys," The first cop said.

"What?"

"Yeah, you think we small-town cops aren't even real cops. I bet you couldn't handle it for a day, city boy."

"Look, I'm a cop just like you, I don't think your job is any easier than mine," Jack protested.

"Oh, that's another thing; you'd better be a real cop. If not, you'll be charged with impersonating a police officer, and carrying a concealed weapon," the first cop said in an angry voice.

"Yeah, you know what the penalty is for impersonating an officer of the law?" the second cop said.

"Oh, man, they won't even have cars by the time you get out; they'll have flying saucers," the first cop said.

Jack was getting angry with these overzealous small-town cops. They threw him against the car with cuffs behind his back. He avoided falling over, but did hurt his head a bit. They were making it clear they didn't like him.

"Fuckin' city cops, think they can just come out here and arrest people anywhere. It's like you think you own the world," the first cop said.

"Listen, these guys Ted and Charlie are killers. I'm just tracking them down, I'm not taking over your town," Jack said.

"You done got that right; you ain't taking over this town. You just better fucking hope you can prove you're a cop, and that these men are Ted and Charlie with fake IDs."

Jack was literally thrown into the police car. They put the other two men into different police cars as gently as could be. On the way back to the police station, Jack felt fidgety. His sick obsession could get him locked up in a redneck county jail. Jack looked at the two men one more time, once again doubting one of them was Ted.

The cops put Jack in a jail cell, and took the other two men to be fingerprinted. Jack felt weird being in a cell; usually he was the one putting people in jail. After a few hours, the arresting officers came to see Jack.

"Well, Mr. Reddick, we've got good news and bad news."

"What?"

"Good news is, your badge came back clean. When you get out, your gun will be issued back to you, and no concealed weapons charges will be brought up against you. The bad news is, the two men you were attempting to arrest are not Ted Amichi or Charlie Fletcher, so you're going to be charged with assault."

This was rock bottom; the two men who had killed his wife were free, while he was in jail.

"Goddamn it, they looked just like them!" Jack said.

"Tell it to the judge," the cop said.

"I thought it was them; I was just doing my job."

"You don't have a job out here; you are not an officer of the law in Oklahoma. You're just some smartass out-of-towner who's in some trouble."

"Can I make my phone call now?"

The cop has a little evil smile on his face. Jack could hear a light chuckle coming from him.

"Phone call? Hmm, you know what, city boy? We don't give phone calls out here."

"The law says I get to make a phone call to arrange bail. How am I supposed to get out of here?"

The cop laughed again.

"Hmm, that's a good question. I hope you can fit through the heating duct, 'cause you ain't leavin' till we say so, and with the way yer acting, it could take a while."

Jack was speechless; he'd really done it this time. The cop walked away, leaving nobody else in the area.

"Just my luck, I get locked up in one of these evil hillbilly jails I used to joke about back home," Jack yelled.

Jack sat there for several hours before anyone even walked by. When the cop came up to Jack's cell, he handed him a bowl of cold oatmeal and a plastic cup of water.

"*Bon appetit*," the cop said.

Jack heard the cop snickering as he walked away. He ate the food, even though it tasted as horrible as it looked. That night, he thought of how much fun it was going to be to wring the necks of Ted and Charlie. It worried him that he might spend a long time sitting in a small-town county jail while Ted might never be brought in.

After two days of sitting in a cell, Jack was dirty and furious. He hadn't even been allowed out to exercise or walk around; he'd been in total isolation. He'd had to sleep on a bunk with no mattress, and felt himself rotting away. His kids were home alone with no mother, and their father was sitting in jail a thousand miles away.

"Maybe when I get out of here I should just forget about

catching those guys. I might as well be dead; I'm never home for the kids," Jack said out loud.

He thought of the days each of his children had been born. He and Peggy had been together and happy as could be. As he was thinking of Peggy it brought a tear to his eyes. He'd always thought he knew Peggy, and tried to think of all the clues he might have missed over the years about her secret life. The memory of the day she was killed came back. Still the image of the killer had not faded.

The next morning, after Jack's cold oatmeal breakfast, he was ready to sleep some more. He tried to get comfortable on the narrow bunk, but it was pointless. There was nothing to do but wonder how long it would be before they let him make a phone call or bail out. Footsteps coming from the hall woke Jack up. The arresting officer and his boss Chief Mahoney were both standing outside his cell. Mahoney must have driven all the way from Utah.

"Jeez, I must be dreaming!" Jack said, laughing for the first time. "Is that you Chief Mahoney?"

"Yes, Jack, I've been driving all night to get here."

The officer opened the cell, and Jack came out to talk to Chief Mahoney. The officer walked away, leaving them alone.

"Did they call you and tell you I was here?" Jack asked.

"Nope, it's a long story how I found you."

"How?"

"When your car was towed, they called the station, since it has Utah police plates on it. I asked where you were. The tow truck guy said he heard you got arrested. So I came down and, sure enough, here you are."

"Those bastards, they didn't even give me a phone call! I've been sitting here for three days with nothing to eat but cold oatmeal."

"I can tell; you look terrible and smell bad, too," Mahoney said.

"Oh, man, why me?"

"Listen, Jack, do you remember last year when you busted one of the biggest drug lords in the state? I told you I owed you one."

"Yes, I do."

"Well, you just used it up, and then some."

"Okay, so how am I gonna get out of here?"

"Well, I got you out and they're dropping the charges."

"How'd you do that?"

"I just pointed out that denying an arrested man his phone call is illegal. If I hadn't tracked you down, God knows how long you would have been here."

"Yeah, I know. They just left me here to die, those hillbillies."

"Well, in exchange for my silence, they've dropped the charges and torn up the arrest report. So, like I said, you owe me a favor now, Jack."

"Yes, I do; thank you."

"Come on, let's get out of here. On the way home I'll think of how you can repay me for this."

Both of them left the station. Jack wanted to tell off the small-town cops, but he realized he just gotten out of trouble and didn't want to get back in. They got into the chief's car and hit the highway.

"So can you pay me the four hundred dollars you owe me this week Jack?" Mahoney said.

"What four hundred dollars?" Jack replied.

"The four hundred dollars it cost me to have your stupid car towed back to Utah."

"Oh, thanks again; I'll get it to you when we get home."

Jack felt tired, hungry and mentally exhausted. He'd seemed so close to catching the killers, as if they'd been in his sights, but he couldn't grab them.

"God, I could use a drink!" Jack said.

"Oh really?"

"Yeah, and a nice big steak dinner, with a big baked potato and lots of butter, along with a couple of scotches."

"Sounds good to me."

"Do they have restaurants in Oklahoma?" Jack said sarcastically.

Mahoney laughed.

"Yeah, I think maybe a few."

Jack opened his wallet. "Goddamn it!"

"What?"

"I had fifty dollars in here; thirty of it's missing."

"Hmm, maybe the redneck cops needed a few drinks, too,"

Mahoney said with a smile.

"Thieves! I hope they use it to buy a noose to hang themselves with!"

Mahoney gave Jack a weird look. They stopped at a steak restaurant. Their waiter's name was Lou. Jack looked at Lou, thinking he looked like a sunflower seed, a farm boy.

"How do ya all do, what can I get for ya?" Lou asked with a loud Southern voice

"I'll have a T-bone cooked—"

"Speak up, man, I can't hear ya," Lou interrupted.

"I said, I'll have a T-bone cooked medium well, with a baked potato and lots of butter. Oh, and a few scotches to go with it," Jack yelled.

The waiter laughed when Jack said he wanted a baked potato.

"I used to work on a tater farm, ya know. One time my stupid friends from Colorado came to my house and tater-bombed it. They broke every window in the house. When I came home there were taters and broken glass all over the livin' room. Let me tell ya, them boys just better hope I never get my hands on 'em," Lou said with chuckle.

Jack and the chief weren't really amused by the waiter's tater-bombing story.

"Anyway, young fella, I'll have a filet mignon and a gin and tonic," Mahoney said.

"You want a tater or coleslaw with that filet?" Lou asked.

"Coleslaw."

Mahoney ordered coleslaw so he wouldn't have to hear any more stories from the waiter.

After a nice meal and good service from a rather strange waiter, they both feel better, especially Jack. While heading toward the door, Jack thought about how nasty the oatmeal had been that they'd served him in jail.

Chapter 6

The New Problem

Jack just wanted to get home and end this rotten road trip. An hour into the journey, though he noticed something odd.

"Hey, chief, that sign said one hundred fifty miles to Texas. We're headed the wrong way; we need to go through Kansas to get to Utah."

"Do we?" Mahoney said with a bit of cleverness in his tone.

"Yeah, we've been driving the wrong way for hours."

"Boy, Jack, it took you this long to realize we're headed the wrong way? You really are the most observant cop on the force."

"Come on, there's an off-ramp; let's just get on home."

"Well, listen, Jackass, I was gonna wait until we got there, or until your dumbass noticed where we are, to tell you something," Mahoney said with a big smile.

Jack was feeling sick and tired, he liked the chief's fun attitude, but just wasn't in the mood to play games. They passed the off-ramp; they needed to turn around.

"Come on, chief, I wanna go home!" Jack said.

"No, you don't."

"Why not?"

"Okay, I'll tell you why, are you sure your ready?"

"Yes, I've been ready for the last five minutes, say it!" Jack grumbled.

"Ted Amichi and Charlie Fletcher were both arrested in Louisiana for auto theft."

Jack went from weary and beat down to excited and energized in a matter of seconds.

"Hey, we got 'em, didn't we?" Jack said.

"Not yet; we have many problems Jack."

Jack was shaky; he didn't want this moment to be ruined by complications.

"What's the problem? Did they escape already?" Jack asked.

"No, Jack, but we need to convince the Louisiana District attorney's office that they should release them to us."

"That should be easy; this was a double murder case."

"No, it's not that easy. Let me explain this to you, Jack. If they release Ted and Charlie, they must drop the auto theft charges against them. Now, we don't even have much of a case against them. Think about it; there was really no motive. You know as well as I do that just because your wife was a counselor from Detroit, isn't enough. Okay, yes, they lived in Detroit, and yeah they might have visited her. But that's not enough for a conviction. Heck, Jack, they might not even make a probable cause hearing."

"I'm a witness. I'll testify; I know it was him."

"Jack, listen, you got a split second view of Ted from over a hundred feet away. Also in a vehicle that was moving over one hundred miles an hour, and that was almost four years ago."

"True, but I know who I saw."

"Oh, really? If you are so damn sure, what was this mess all about here, with you beating up and arresting the wrong guy?"

"It was an accident. I panicked; I flipped, but later I realized it wasn't them."

"Come on, Jack, there is no proof that these men had any prior contact with your wife. She destroyed all evidence of her being in Detroit. She's dead, and you're not a credible witness, especially since you are the husband; that will make you a biased witness."

Jack realized that catching the killers was only the beginning of a long horrible mess. All these years he'd thought once he caught them, it was a done deal; they'd go straight to the chair.

"Down in Louisiana, they can for sure convict them of auto theft. Why would they give that up for a long-shot chance of a murder conviction in Utah?"

"We're screwed, huh? They're just gonna get away with two first-degree murders, aren't they?"

"I don't know."

"Well, after they're done serving their time, can't we at least try to get them?"

"Well, no, we have to do this now. We have one thing on our side, and we need to hurry."

"What's that?"

"Well, Mrs. Lipan, the teacher at the school got a good look at Ted when he entered the school. He had sunglasses on, but she got a good look at him, unlike you."

"Is that enough to get 'em to release them?"

"I hope so, 'cause that old woman had a stroke a few months ago, and she's dying. If we don't get her into court to finger them before she dies, then we have about nothing."

"What about the junkyard guys?"

"Well, we could only use them if Ted and Charlie were convicted of the vandalism. They weren't, and making a case could take years. Mrs. Lipan is probably not gonna make it to the end of this year."

"God, this just gets worse and worse," Jack said.

"Well, I just hope we can convince the District Attorney that we have a good enough case against Ted and Charlie, so they will released them to us. Maybe we could force Louisiana to release them, but that could take a while. It's best if we can just get some cooperation."

"Yeah," Jack said.

"All we have is Mrs. Lipan; you're not credible. The junkyard guys aren't any good, so we have one hope, Jack."

They reached the jail where Ted and Charlie were being held. As they were walking in, Jack was in a whole different world. Jack panicked at the fact that the county jail looked like someone's old farm.

"I can't believe those guys are here; I've been tracking them for years, and finally here they are," he said.

"Jack, just concentrate on what you're going to say, okay?"

They met with the District Attorney, John Cooley. As soon as

Jack saw Cooley, he thought, There's no way this guy will release them. Just by looking at Cooley's cocky grin and custom-tailored thousand-dollar suit he knew this guy was trouble. Cooley's spiked, gelled hair, his nice build and clean white face just screamed "egomaniac."

"So, you guys think ole' Ted and Charlie here are the murderers you're looking for?" Cooley said.

"Yes, we have proof," Mahoney said.

"Well, this better be good, 'cause I can easily convict them on charges of auto theft. You better convince me that I should let them go."

"Well, you said in your report you found a .45 handgun on them. In our case, one victim was shot with a .45," Mahoney said.

"Yeah well, that's not really enough," Cooley said.

"Well, I was an eye witness when the men were running, and I'd like to look at them," Jack said.

"Fine, let's go to their cell," Cooley said.

Jack was trembling and felt as if little needles were poking him. Finally he was going to come face to face with the man he had ruined his life to find. They arrived at the cell. Cooley snapped his fingers.

"Ted, get over here, we want to look at you," he said.

Ted got up and came to the front of the cell. Jack and Ted looked at each other for the first time in four long, agonizing years. Ted knew who Jack was, but looked at him with no expression, as if Jack was a total stranger. Inside, Ted was screaming from all sides; he knew what was going on, but had to act as if it was nothing.

"That's definitely him," Jack said.

"Okay, let's go," Cooley said.

When Jack saw Ted he didn't see a man, he saw the four years of hell he went through to get him. Jack couldn't find one guard around to stop Ted if he tried to escape. Jack had a momentary thought that he should shoot Ted right now, so he wouldn't risk a jailbreak. They went back to the office and everyone took a seat.

"Look, I've read these police reports that were faxed to me. I don't believe you're a credible witness, Jack," Cooley said.

"I know who I saw," Jack said.

"Jack, you only saw him for a second at one hundred mph, and that was four years ago. Come on, you're just wanting someone to pay for this so you can rest."

"Wrong! I want to find the man who really did it. I wouldn't say it was him if I wasn't 100% sure it was him."

"Mr. Cooley," Mahoney interrupted. "We have a teacher at the school that saw him when he entered. She's dying; we need to get her into court before she goes."

Cooley still wasn't budging. It wasn't that he didn't think Utah had a chance; it was more about his monster ego, and needing the conviction in his own state. He was almost getting an erection from having these two guys sucking up to him.

"Look, you know as well as I do that an old woman's testimony isn't enough, either. According to the report, she didn't see his face; he had a helmet on and sunglasses," Cooley said.

"I know, but we have me as a witness, Mrs. Lipan, and maybe the junkyard guys," Jack reasoned. "The handgun itself, and the circumstantial evidence that he lived in the city where my wife worked. It may be enough, and in a trial anything can happen."

"Yeah, I know anything can happen, like maybe they'll be found not guilty and we'll waste our chance to for sure convict them of auto theft. Then I'm gonna look like a damn fool!" Cooley said.

"I'm telling you, we can get them to break. We'll find something. I've spent four years finding them. I'll do what it takes to get 'em. You won't be sorry," Jack promised.

Cooley pondered for a moment. His erection got bigger as Jack put more and more begging in his tone.

"You willing to bet your career on that, Jack?" Cooley asked.

"I would, if I could."

Cooley smiled with his perfect bleached white teeth showing, as he turned to the chief.

"Okay, Chief Mahoney, here's what I'll do. I'll release them to Utah for the murder trial. But in the contract I sign, if they're found not guilty, Jack must be fired for embarrassing the justice system."

"Well, Jack, what do you say? Will you put your job on the

line?" Mahoney asked.

Jack thought about it for a moment. If he said yes it could speed up the process and have a better chance of a conviction. If he said no, it would be fun to crush Cooley's ego, but Mrs. Lipan might die and the more he looked at this county jail, the more it scared him. The security around there was pathetic at best. Although he was a smart man, his obsession to find his wife's killer had already made him do dumb things. He knew he didn't have to take Cooley's offer. The thought of how easy it would be for Ted to escape from this jail if Cooley didn't release him made the decision easy.

"Sure, if I can't get a murder conviction on Ted and Charlie, I'll accept being fired for embarrassing you."

"Well, then, I'll drop my charges and have him sent out to Utah," Cooley said.

"We're headed that way, why don't you just let him ride back there with us?" Jack said.

Cooley laughed for almost twenty seconds. His laugh was overdramatized just to intimidate Jack and Mahoney more.

"Not on your life, Jack! I'll arrange for them to be flown out there next week," Cooley said.

"That'll be fine," Mahoney said.

"Well, you'd better not embarrass me, Jack," Cooley said.

"I won't; I'll find a way to convince a jury of their guilt."

"Yeah, you better."

"Yep, no question."

"Oh, one more thing to help you out. You can use the junkyard guys as witnesses, if they're willing to drop the vandalism charges," Cooley said.

"Oh, really?" Jack replied.

"Yes, but if those boys are still wanting to press charges, then Ted and Charlie won't have to answer a question about the pending case in a Utah court, because it would be considered a conflict of interest."

"Hmm," Jack mumbled.

"It's true, if they also drop their charges against them, it would be a closed case and they could be used as witnesses."

"Well, I guess the chief and I have one more stop before home."

"I'm sure we can convince them to drop their charges as well, so they can help us," Mahoney said.

"Well, good luck to you all, especially you, Jack," Cooley said looking Jack right in the eye.

Cooley's hot babe secretary walked in. She almost broke one of her inch-long red fingernails on the door.

"Hey, baby, would you go get me some prisoner release forms?" Cooley smiled at her. "Oh, and escort these two gentlemen out the door."

"Sure thing," she replied.

"Oh, one more thing, babe. Don't wear sneakers to work tomorrow, I like high heels."

She didn't say anything in response; instead she escorted Jack and Mahoney out. As she passed by Cooley, he slapped her lightly on her cute little butt. She didn't do much about it. It seemed she was used to it.

"Boy, you're willing to put your job on the line for this thing, you really must want it," Mahoney said to Jack on the way out.

"Yes, I do. I know it's risky, but I'll kick myself if I blow my one chance to finally get Ted Amichi. I mean, come on, to force Cooley to extradite Ted could take months. By then Ted could escape, I'm surprised he hasn't already, the security around here is horrendous. I wanna get him back to Utah where I can watch him 24-7."

"I hope you can be just as convincing in Oklahoma as you were here."

"Yeah, I'm sure those boys'll drop the charges, especially if they can help us fry Ted and Charlie."

They took turns driving, but it still took them eight hours to get back to the junkyard in Oklahoma. When they arrived, they were both exhausted. They decided to stay at a motel for the night and talk to the junkyard boys tomorrow. The next morning, Jack went to the yard with Mahoney.

"I really hate bothering these guys again; I'm sure they're quite busy," Jack said.

Mahoney noticed ten empty Budweiser bottles on the ground,

not including the six empty cans from the last time Jack was here.

"Yeah, right, we're probably the only ones who've been here since Ted and Charlie," Mahoney said.

"Hope my plan works," Jack said.

"What's your plan?"

"Oh, you'll see."

They met Bud and Eddie outside. Both of them had beers in their hands.

"Hey, did you catch those sons of bitches yet?" Eddie asked.

"As a matter of fact, we did," Jack said.

"What! Where are they?" Eddie yelled.

"They're being taken back to Utah to stand trial for two first-degree murders."

"Forget that," Eddie said. "Just let me take care of them."

"I take it that they're not going to pay us for what they did?" Bud interrupted.

"Well, yes," Jack said with a wink to Mahoney. "That's about right."

"So they're just gonna get away with it, huh?" Eddie said as he lit up a cigarette.

"Well, there is one way to get compensated for your damages," Jack said slowly.

"What might that be?" Bud asked as he took a swig of beer.

"I need you guys to testify in the Utah court about what these men did and said to you."

"Utah's kinda far," Bud said.

"No, first I want them to pay us for what they did here," Eddie said as he blew smoke out of his nose. "Then I'll testify."

Jack was getting irate, but he didn't want to tick these guys off.

"Okay, here's my one offer; listen carefully. You'll never get any money out of these guys, because even if they don't get convicted of murder in Utah, other states will get them. But it'll be years before you ever even get a chance. I'll make you one offer," Jack said.

"What's the offer?" Bud asked.

"Okay, now please listen carefully. I personally will compensate you for the car Ted wrecked. In exchange, you must drop the charges against these men. Once you drop the charges, then you must act as witnesses in court as to what they said."

"So we have to drop the charges?" Bud said.

"Yep."

"Hell with that, I want them to pay for what they did to us," Eddie said.

"Forget this petty charge; if you help me convict them of murder, they could get the chair, and you'll for sure get your money from me," Jack said.

Bud and Eddie looked at each other. Eddie threw his cigarette on the ground. Bud looked at Jack.

"Fine, we'll drop the charges and appear in Utah as witnesses. But not only do I want the money that we lost, I want a front row seat when they fry that son of a bitch," Bud said.

"Sure, but that will only happen if I can get a case against them."

"Deal," Bud said.

"Okay, please keep this deal quiet, we could all get in trouble if the D.A. were to find out that I paid you guys," Jack said.

"Sure, we'll shut up, just tell us when and where we need to go," Bud said.

"I will have you flown out to Utah when you are needed. Also I'll have the D.A.'s office mail you some forms. Just sign them and that will be that."

They all shook hands.

"Boy, Jack, you're putting your career, your life, and all your money on this thing," Mahoney said.

"I have to; it's the only way."

Chapter 7

The Trial

After a long, boring trip Jack and Mahoney finally made it home. Jack was happy to see his neglected kids again. Over the next month, Jack tried to save every penny he could. This way, he would have money for his kids, in case he was to lose his job. Ted and Charlie were extradited to Utah and arrested on two counts of first-degree murder. It was decided that they would both be tried together on the charges. Sure enough, both men pleaded not guilty.

On the first day of the trial, Jack was a wreck. He'd dreamed of this day for years, but he was worried these guys would get away with it. Both Jack and Ted had their whole lives on the line with this trial.

Ted and Charlie's lawyer was a woman named Mary Lange. Although she was a mean, witty, stuck-up snappy bitch, Ted liked her. Even Charlie was turned on by this tall, anorexic successful lady, in her tight reveling black business suit. Her black plastic 70's style glasses with their rectangle lenses, along with the right amount of make-up and lipstick, gave her a smart look. This was definitely not the kind of lawyer Jack wanted defending these guys. [Ted and Charlie's request to have a judge trial instead of a jury trial, because of the publicity around town was granted, thank to Mary's outstanding ability to get what she wants.]

The prosecutor in this case was Nick Bowling, or Tricky Nicky. Jack wasn't impressed by this nickname; he just wanted him to convict Ted and Charlie.

"All rise for the honorable Judge Norton Foster," the bailiff said.

The elderly teacher, Mrs. Lipan was the first witness called. The first thing everyone noticed was the oxygen tank that she wheeled behind her.

"Do you recognize the man you saw at the school that day?" Nick asked her.

"Yes, I do," Mrs. Lipan said.

"Will you point him out, please?" She pointed right at Ted. "Let the record show that the witness has identified Theodore Amichi. No more questions, Your Honor."

Jack clenched his fists at the sight of Mary Lange getting up for her turn. Her red high heels made the usual loud clicking noises as she walked across the marble floor of the courtroom.

"Ma'am, would you mind telling the court your age?" Mary asked.

"I'm seventy-six."

"So you were seventy-two years old when this happened?"

"Yes."

"I see that you wear glasses, and that you're very ill."

"Yes."

"Now, you said, and the police reports say, that the man was wearing sunglasses and a helmet. You yourself didn't even talk to the man. He walked right past you. And this was four years ago."

"Yes."

"I want you to look at this paper," Mary said as she handed Mrs. Lipan the paper, which had photos of six different faces; each of which looked like Ted Amichi.

"Study that for a moment," Mary said.

Mrs. Lipan looked at all the pictures. Some of the men had long hair, others had the crew cut. One photo had a young man, while the other had an older man. They all could be Ted. Mary took the paper away after a few minutes.

"Okay, which one of these photos is Ted Amichi?" Mary said holding up a larger version of the six photos.

"Number five, I believe," Mrs. Lipan said.

Mary smirked as she swung her shiny blonde hair around her shoulders.

"Are you sure that's him?" Mary said, followed by a smile.

"Yes, I believe so."

"Your Honor, I'd ask you to look at this. Ted is sitting in the courtroom right now. Yet, the witness still picked the wrong photo. Ted is the first photo. How can she be sure that Ted Amichi was the man she saw in sunglasses four years ago? She can't even tell a photo of a man whose sitting right in front of her. Defense asks that her statement be dismissed."

Nick looked at the photo sheet. He assumed the Ted photo must be from the 70's.

"Request denied," Judge Foster said.

Nick decided not to fight the fact that the photo was twenty years old, since Mrs. Lipan's testimony was still good; it might irate Judge Foster.

"No more questions, Your Honor," Mary said.

At the prosecution's table, Nick leaned over to Jack.

"Oh, no, she was our best defense, and that bitch just shot her down," Nick said.

Jack nodded and wished the roof would cave in and kill him, so he wouldn't have to deal with this. Next it was his turn to take the stand.

"Mr. Reddick, when you and Officer Rosen were chasing the two men that day, did you got a look at the gunman himself?" Nick asked after Jack had been sworn in.

"Yes, and I'll add that his helmet and sunglasses had fallen off. So I got a complete view of the man's face."

"Very well. Is the man that you saw in this courtroom today?"

"Yes," Jack said as he pointed right at Ted Amichi.

"Let the record show that Sergeant Reddick has identified the defendant, Theodore Amichi. I have no further questions."

Mary had completely browbeaten Mrs. Lipan, but Jack wasn't going to let her get to him.

"Mr. Reddick, forgive my skepticism, but according to the report, you only got a split-second view of the shooter, who was shooting at you from a vehicle traveling one hundred miles per hour. How can you say with absolute certainty four years later that

Theodore Amichi was the man you saw?" Mary asked.

"I can say it because I know he was the man I saw."

Mary turned away from Jack and approached Judge Foster's bench. "Your Honor, I would like to ask the six police officers in the back row to stand up."

Jack had wondered why there were six cops in the courtroom that day. He'd figured it was for security.

"You haven't seen Officer Bundy in four years, have you, Mr. Reddick?"

"No, I was in the car with Officer Rosen. I only saw Officer Bundy when I stopped to pick up Officer Rosen," Jack replied, guessing where this was going.

"Yes, I know; I've done my homework. But you did see Officer Bundy briefly that day, correct?"

"Yes, I saw him when I picked up Rosen to go chase the fleeing suspects."

"Of these six officers in the back row, which one is Officer Bundy?"

"Objection!" Nick said.

"These officers are too far away; they need to be moved closer."

"Overruled," Judge Foster said. "They're close enough for Sergeant Reddick to see their faces."

Jack looked closely. Every one of them looked the same with their blue uniform, cop mustache and crew cut. Jack knew he didn't remember Officer Bundy, but definitely remembered Ted, and that this would look critical.

"He's third from the left," Jack said.

"Incorrect," Mary said sharply. "Officer Bundy, would you raise your hand, please?"

The second man from the right raised his hand.

"Thank you," Mary said, and all six men took their seats again. "Your Honor, I submit that Mr. Reddick's testimony lacks credibility. If he can't identify someone with whom he had contact that day, how could he remember Theodore Amichi? He only saw him for a split-second, even further away then these six men are from him now, in a car going one hundred mph."

"It's true I remember Theodore Amichi because he's the man who killed my wife!" Jack objected. "I didn't remember Bundy, because he wasn't meaningful to me that day."

"It shows your memory isn't clear. No more questions, Your Honor," Mary said.

Jack left the stand. Two eyewitnesses had been shot down, and he was one of them. The only hope was the junkyard guys.

To Jack's surprise, Eddie and Bud were wearing suits and ties; they actually looked good.

"According to the police report, after a man smashed your car to bits, he aimed a .45 handgun at you? Is that true?" Nick asked Eddie.

"Yes."

"What did they say to you?"

"The man holding the handgun to my face said that I had better not fuck with him. He said he had killed two people before and one of them was a cop," Eddie said.

"Did you get a good look at these men?"

"Yes, I did," Eddie said.

"Would you point out the men that you saw?"

Eddie pointed out Ted and Charlie. Nick asked him to step down, then asked Bud the same questions and got the same responses.

"Your Honor, both of these men have identified Theodore Amichi and Charles Fletcher as being the men they saw at their junkyard. No sunglasses, no helmets. They got a great look at them because they chatted with them for over twenty minutes about a transmission. These two witnesses have actually talked to the men and also identified a .45 handgun aimed at them. Mr. Amichi had a .45 handgun in his car when he was arrested. Also, I might add that a .45 handgun was used to kill Peggy Reddick. I have no further questions."

Nick's attitude was confident; he didn't know how Mary could shoot this down. To Nick and Jack's surprise, she seemed very confident as she approached Bud on the witness stand.

"You're so certain that these two men are the same men you saw at the yard?" Mary said.

"Yes, ma'am," Bud answered.

"Did you actually hear either of these men say 'I killed Peggy Reddick and Officer Marshall?" she asked.

"No, ma'am."

"Did they even say that the murders were in Utah?"

"No. The guy had a gun aimed at my partner's face, so I didn't ask for specific details about the murders," Bud said.

"As I understand it," Mary said slowly. "No one pulled a gun until after your partner refused to refund the five hundred dollars for a job he was unable to do. So you were ripping these guys off and they got mad and retaliated against you. You then report that you shut the gates and threatened to kill them for wrecking your car. So it would be safe to say that they probably were scared to death, and said the first thing that came to their minds, so you would let them leave."

"No, ma'am," Bud said. "If they had worked with us, we would've called the sheriff and resolved it. But since he had a gun to our faces, we did what we had to do."

"Do you know that if you have killed Ted or Charlie that day, you would be the one on trial right now?"

"We had no intention of killing them," Bud said.

"Oh, but we don't know that, do we?" Mary asked. "You're crooks, you're violent, and any reasonable man would do what was needed to get out of there, even if it meant making up a story that they had killed people."

Nick was on his feet. "Objection! Your Honor, who in their right mind would say 'I killed a cop and another person' in such a situation? Ms. Lange is badgering the witness."

"Overruled," the judge said.

"No further questions," Mary said.

The court took a recess. Jack found Nick in the lobby; they needed to talk.

"Well, Eddie and Bud's testimony helped, but I can't say that will seal the case," Nick said.

"Do we have anything else?" Jack asked.

"Just the .45, but ballistics weren't conclusive," Nick replied.

Jack lowered his head in disgust.

The trial went on for a few more days. During this time, questions focused on the gun. Mary pointed out that the gun was legal and there was no way to trace that particular .45 as the weapon used. She also cast doubts on Jack and Laura's testimony about Peggy's secret life in Detroit.

Finally Ted Amichi was called to the stand.

"He doesn't even look like a killer," Nick whispered to Jack. "He actually looks like a nice guy."

"Yep, he does, but little does anyone know what he's capable of," Jack replied.

"Jack, I must also tell you that neither of these guys even has a criminal record," Nick said.

Jack didn't want to accept it, but he was sure that Ted and Charlie were going to walk.

"I know, I find it hard to believe they're killers, why did they target Peggy?" Jack said.

"Yeah, they're clean-cut, good looking, and except for that scar on Ted's cheek, he looks perfect," Nick replied.

Jack hadn't noticed the scar on Ted's face, but sure enough, there it was. Jack wondered why he hadn't noticed it before. He'd studied the picture of Ted that he'd gotten from GM and never noticed the scar. Jack looked through his briefcase and pulled out the photo of Ted from GM. It was clear why he never noticed the scar. It was because Ted hadn't had the scar when the photo was taken. Jack noticed the photo had been taken only months before Peggy's murder. That meant Ted got the scar after this photo was taken.

Jack went over the day of the murder again. He remembered every detail of the chase and about Ted. He'd read the police reports filed by Officer Rosen after the chase. In the report it said that Jack had shot out the passenger window of the Cadillac. The man wasn't shot, but the glass shattered in his face. Jack remembered shooting at Ted, and how disappointed he had been that he'd missed.

Then it hit him--the scar on Ted's face was from the shattering glass. He quickly explained his findings to Nick. Both of them got excited.

"This could be it," Nick said. He stood up, full of energy.

"Mr. Amichi, I'd first like to ask you if you lived in Detroit in 1999?" Nick asked.

"Yes, I did," Ted replied.

"Did you and your wife ever see a marriage counselor?"

"No, we never did."

"Ever been to Utah?"

"Nope, this trial is the first time."

"I see that you own a .45 handgun."

"Yes, I do."

"Why do you have it?"

"Well, Detroit can be a hard place to live in with all the gangs. So I bought it for protection."

"Mr. Amichi, I see that you have a scar on your cheek. How did you get that?"

"Oh, I got it at work, because I worked in manufacturing cars."

"Was it from glass?"

"I believe so; I worked in the glass and body shop, and it can be very dangerous."

"How long ago?"

"Oh a while."

"A while. Was it five years? Ten years? Twenty years? Tell me how long ago."

"I'd say 1991."

Nick smiled.

"Your Honor, I have here a picture of Ted Amichi that was taken in early 1999, only a few months before the murder. As you can see, he has no scar on his cheek."

Nick handed Judge Foster the photo.

"Objection, this has no relevance to the case," Mary said.

"Overruled," Foster said, studying the photo. "Make your point, Mr. Bowling."

"Well, Your Honor, the police report indicates that the passenger side window of the suspects' car was shot out and the glass shattered in the gunman's face. Ted Amichi has not only been fingered as the man with the gun, but he has the scars on his face, to prove that the glass shattered in his face. The photo you're holding was taken just before Mr. Amichi was fired from the GM plant where he claims to have gotten the scar. There is no indication of a scar in the photo."

Nick turned back to Ted. "Why would you lie about that scar, Mr. Amichi? The only reason to lie would be if you had something to hide. Like the truth, that you're the man who killed Peggy Reddick and Officer Marshall, then bragged about it at the junkyard. No further questions," Nick added before Ted could even answer.

Mary was disquieted in her turn, she was behind and had a lot of explaining to do.

"Ted, do you actually remember getting the scar?" Mary asked.

"No, I think it was at work."

"Your Honor, they came up with a great story of the glass shattering on the gunman. But keep in mind, Ted never said an exact time. Who could remember when they got a scar? It could have been 1999 instead of 1991. Ted didn't lie, he just didn't know. Also, the picture they have was a security card picture. It was very possible, Ted wore makeup over the scar so he would look good for the picture. This was just a desperate attempt by the prosecution, because they know they have no case. Nothing further," Mary said.

After closing arguments Judge Foster turned in. Only time would decide Jack and Ted's fate.

"Well Jack, I'm not sure if it'll be enough, but soon we'll see," Nick said.

Judge Foster reached a verdict in two days. Just before reading it, Jack closed his eyes and crossed his fingers. So did Ted, even though Ted's hoping for a different verdict than Jack was.

"Would the defendants please rise," Foster said.

"I find the defendants Theodore Amichi and Charlie Fletcher; Guilty of two counts of murder in the first degree."

Neither Ted nor Charlie moved a muscle, even when Mary talked to Ted about an appeal. Ted didn't care one bit, he knew appeals were rarely successful. Ted and Charlie spoke for a few minutes to each other. All anybody heard was Charlie saying, "go ahead Ted, tell 'em."

"Mr. Amichi, do you have anything to say before sentencing?" Foster asked.

"I think I should tell now," Ted replied.

"Ted no!" Mary shouted.

"I want to tell! Your honor, Mr. Reddick, Andy, Nita, if you are willing to sit for the next two hours, I'll tell everything right now."

"Yes, tell us Ted," Jack shouted.

"Mr. Reddick, please be quite! Okay Ted, I got nothing but time, start at the beginning tell us everything," Foster said.

"Are you sure?"

"Yes, I myself think this is extremely weird. Why would you just pick someone out, and murder them for no reason? Are you sick?" Foster asked.

"No, I'm not sick. Oh boy, here it goes. I remember my first real good job interview in 1976. Getting this job would be the beginning of my success and downfall," Ted said.

Chapter 8

Ted's Story Begins

"After reviewing your application, I've decided to accept you for the position," Benny Stone the personnel director said.

"Oh wow, I don't know what to say!" Ted Amichi grinned.

When Benny said the word "accept," relief washed over Ted in an awesome way. It was already intimidating enough that Benny was head of his own department and only fifteen years older then Ted. If he hadn't gotten the job, he'd have felt like wearing a bag over his head.

At twenty-three years old, six feet tall, one hundred eighty pounds, Ted was strikingly good looking. Benny Stone's secretary couldn't stop staring at him from the outer office. It was unclear whether it was Ted's ultra-shiny almost shoulder-length hair, or if it was his clean, slightly tanned face with the thin colorless lips that was turning her on. Ted ran his finger inside the back of his collar. He felt a rash developing around his neck from wearing the only suit he owned. The summer heat and the rash were yet another constant reminder of why he hated dressing up. The suit looked great on him, but if he could have worn ragged clothes, he would have.

Benny signed the application and dated it June 2, 1976.

"This isn't your ordinary job, Ted," he pointed out. "Most don't get hired, but your experience and skills gave you the winning edge. I'm putting you on fenders and glass."

"I'm very honored," Ted said.

"It's no rumor, Cadillacs and GM are the best American cars money can buy. They're the American dream; when you're making these great cars, in reality you'll be making the American dream,"

Benny said as he laughed.

Ted laughed as well, in a poor attempt to imitate Benny.

"You'll start at ten dollars an hour. As a benefit, you get either an extra fifty cents an hour, or once a year you can have a new Cadillac at the manufacturer's price. That's about one-third the dealer price," Benny said.

"I'll want the new Caddy' in fact I have fallen in love with the brand new Seville models."

"Okay, I'll put you down for a new one. You start tomorrow, eight to four."

"Great. Once again, thank you," Ted said.

Ted left and went straight to Barney's, his favorite bar and grill. There he met his best friend Charlie Fletcher. He and Charlie looked enough alike to be brothers.

"Hey, Charlie, how'd your interview go?" Ted asked.

"I got it! I'm now in construction," Charlie said.

"Good going."

"Well, how 'bout you? Are you gonna build Cadillacs?"

"Yep, and I'm gonna get a new car also."

"Really? You sure as hell need a new car! What are you gonna get?"

"Well, since I now work for Cadillac, I'm gonna get a brand-new '76 six Seville at manufacturer's cost."

The other guys at the bar turn to talk to Ted. None of them could imagine Ted in a Cadillac.

"A Cadillac, wow; you can't get a better car," Marty the bartender said.

"I know; my old '62 Chevy is more than shot," Ted replied.

"What color you gonna get?" Charlie asked.

"Light blue, with white leather seats. Brand-new, my first brand-new car," Ted said.

"Well, Ted, looks like we both have great days ahead. I was actually thinking of buying a new car, since I now have a higher paying job," Charlie said.

Ted nodded his head and smiled. For once he couldn't wait to go to work the next morning.

"Hey, Marty, two beers, please," Ted said.

"Hey, everyone, I'm taking bets on the basketball game. Who's in?" Marty asked.

"Ten dollars here," one of the guys yelled.

"Twenty here," Ted yelled.

"I don't know if I should," Charlie said.

"Oh, come on, Charlie! You don't think our good old Detroit Pistons can beat the lousy Lakers?"

"Well, probably. Hey, Marty, twenty here."

After three beers each, Ted and Charlie left.

"Well, good luck on your first day," Charlie said.

"Same to you," Ted replied.

The next morning Ted went to work early. He got the hang of things easily. Everyone was really impressed with Ted's ability to run machinery he has never been trained on. Ted was a hands-on person, the type who would not read instructions, just use a thing and figure it out.

After eight weeks on the job, Ted had enough money to buy his new car.

"Hello, Mr. Stone," Ted said.

"Hello, Ted; I heard you're really busting some ass," Benny said.

"Oh, yes, in fact I've saved enough, I think I can buy that '76 Seville I wanted."

"Good going; just write me a check, and by the end of the week it'll be in the parking lot waiting for you. You'll probably be putting the fenders on your own car, so make sure you are on top of things this week."

Ted wrote him a check for $3,300, just about every cent he had saved up, and they went through the paperwork. Benny knew all the methods of selling a car directly from the manufacturer. After he signed over the title, it was a done deal.

The next morning Ted was working hard to prove to Benny Stone what he was made of. He knew this was the type of company that rewarded hard workers. In the past, employers had punished good workers like him by making them work harder than everyone else. No matter what, he wasn't going to let bad jobs from the past ruin his good job now.

After three months on the job, Ted was given a fifty cent an hour raise. This wasn't company policy. Stone just wanted to reward Ted with this raise to keep him on the team.

On a Saturday in early November, Ted went over to Charlie's place, where he found his friend hard at work wiping down his brand-new '76 Mustang. There were falling leaves everywhere and the combinations of foliage and slight chill made it a typical November day.

"Well, aren't we cool, with our new cars," Ted said as he approached Charlie.

"Hell, yeah! Wanna race?"

"No way; I'm not interested in ruining my brand-new car."

"Oh, well, I'd've won anyway."

"Says you," Ted said as he laughed. "How was your Halloween?"

"Well, those goddamn kids smashed a pumpkin in my driveway."

"Little brats; I hope they all enjoyed the cheap candy I handed out," Ted said as he laughed.

"At least they didn't touch my new car," Charlie said.

"Oh, yeah, I forgot to tell you, I got four-fifty for my old car."

"Wow, what are you gonna to do with all that money?"

"Well, after Christmas I plan to buy one of the new '77 Caddys that I make."

"Are you gonna trade in the '76?"

"No, I love this thing; I'll just have two Caddys."

"Do you really need two brand-new cars?"

"No, but why not? I've been poor my whole life. I've never had a new car or a good job. Ya know, I say, fuck it, now that I got the good job, and only have to pay one-third the price, why not buy two?" Ted said.

"Groovy. Twice the fun. Hey, I have to shower. Wanna meet at the grill in two hours?"

"Sure, see you there, Mustang man."

At the bar, he and Charlie each ordered two shots of Jagermeister.

"This shit's expensive; how come you have money to burn, Teddy?' Marty asked.

"I got a fifty cent an hour raise. Besides I'm not gonna live like a bum anymore; those days are over," Ted replied.

"Oh, good, now I can charge you fifty cents more per beer!" Marty said with a laugh.

Ted smiled, hoping Marty wasn't serious.

After two hours, Ted and Charlie left. Walking across the parking lot, they talked about the holidays.

"Where do you want to have Christmas this year?" Charlie asked.

"Well, last Christmas you and your family came over to my mother's place, so me and my family should come to your family's place this year."

"Okay, I'll see you there. My mother was so excited about seeing your new car; she didn't believe me when I told her what you bought," Charlie said.

"She'll believe it when she sees it."

"It will be nice to get out of my neighborhood for a while."

"Man, Charlie, your apartment is better than mine; that place is fallin' to pieces."

"Well, at least my mother's house doesn't have a rat problem, like my apartment does," Charlie said.

When Christmas came around, Ted was more than ready for some time off. He drove his Mother to Charlie's family's house in the Cadillac.

"There he is," Charlie said to his mother Carol and father Richard.

Charlie's parents looked like happy retired elderly people with their outdated clothes, a tobacco pipe in dad's mouth, both gray haired and an average house in the suburbs. As Charlie looked at Ted's mother Susan, he couldn't see the happy old woman that he saw in his own mother. Susan did everything to look as young as she could. Her dyed hair and modern clothes that teenagers wore, suggested that she was single and looking, while still in the working world.

"My God, the neighbors are gonna think we won the lottery," Carol replied, seeing the car.

"Hey, Charlie! Man, what a relief it is to be here," Ted said when he came up to the door.

"I hope you enjoy my cooking," Carol said.

"Heck, yeah, I always do," Ted replied.

All the food was on the table and everyone was seated. They all bowed their heads for a prayer. After the prayer, they ate and conversed with each other.

"So, Teddy, tell us about your job," Charlie's dad Richard said.

"Well, by the first of the month we will be completely done building the 1977 models."

"That must be an accomplishment," Carol said.

"I wanna buy one of the new '77 models," Ted said.

"What about your new '76?" Richard asked.

"Oh, I'm gonna keep it, but there's nothing like having two cars, and with the discount I got I can really afford it."

"Well, Ted you do only live once, so I'd say what the heck, go for it," Carol said.

"Oh, my, Ted, why do you want to waste your money? Cars are a terrible investment," Ted's mother Susan said.

"Oh, Mom, come on! We never even had close to a new car growing up. Heck, we couldn't buy a car unless it was beat up and sitting on the side of the road."

"That's why you should save your money, in case a rainy day comes."

"Well, Mom, I will, but just for once I want to be careless, just blow my money, and actually feel like I'm an important person. Like there's no tomorrow."

"Oh, Ted, don't do that!"

Ted smiled just to avoid an argument with his mother on the holidays. He knew no matter what, she would be stuck in her old ways of saving every nickel. Ted knew that she didn't really know him too well.

After dinner and dessert, everyone was stuffed.

"Oh boy, I haven't had a meal like that for a while," Ted said.

"Yeah, we usually have beer and bar peanuts for dinner," Charlie added.

"Your cooking was wonderful," Susan said to Carol.

"Yep, if that was my last meal, I'd tell the warden to bring on the electric chair," Ted said.

Charlie and Ted laughed. Their parents didn't really approve of their dark humor.

"So, who's up for a game of Monopoly?" Charlie said.

"Okay, but after the table is cleared," Carol said.

They all cleared the table. Carol poured everybody a glass of red wine to go with the game. Ted beat everybody, but it was close between him and Charlie. After the game, it was time to go to bed.

"Guys, just make yourselves at home; you know where the guest bedrooms are," Carol said to Ted and Charlie.

The next morning Ted and Charlie woke up refreshed. It felt weird that it was a weekday and they weren't working.

"So who wants to help cook New Year's dinner next week?" Susan asked.

"That's women's work," Ted replied.

"Oh, really? Didn't you and Charlie cook at the Michigan Steakhouse for a few years?" Susan asked.

"Yes, we did," Charlie replied.

"But that's a restaurant; it's different than home," Ted said.

"God, Ted you're just like your father, still thinking it's the 1920's," Susan said.

"You know, that's really funny," Carol interrupted so Ted and Susan wouldn't argue.

"What is?" Charlie asked.

"Well, at restaurants it's always tradition that men cook. Yet in the home, it's tradition that women cook," Carol said.

"Hmm," Ted said.

"That is sort of strange," Charlie agreed.

"You know what? At the restaurant, me and Charlie made a killer Key lime pie," Ted said.

"Yeah, I think it was our desserts that kept the line out the door on weekends," Charlie added.

"Of course, the manager didn't agree. Even though when we left the place went to hell with the new cooks. That was a horrible job, especially since we only made minimum wage," Ted said.

"I can't believe that stupid kid still ratted on us for stealing the beer, even though we paid him off," Charlie said.

"What!" Susan said. "Ted, you told me you got laid off from that job."

"Well, don't just talk, show us what you got. The limes are in the left bottom door of the refrigerator, make us a key lime pie," Carol said to interrupt Ted and Susan.

The following week, everything went well for New Year's dinner. Just as Ted had bragged, everyone loved the Key lime pie. For New Year's Eve, Carol bought a special bottle of Merlot.

"So, Ted and Charlie, what are your New Year's resolutions?" Carol asked.

"I just wanna make it through another year," Ted said.

"Ditto. You know, I really don't want to go back to work on Tuesday," Charlie said.

"Well, it won't be so bad for me," Ted said.

"Why is that?" Charlie asked.

"Because I get my new Cadillac on Tuesday."

"I still don't see why you need two cars, son," Susan said.

"One minute to go till 1978," Carol interrupted, so Ted and his mother wouldn't argue about the car.

The next morning Ted and Charlie were watching *Sheriff Lobo* on television. Both in pajamas, eating day old turkey and drinking some leftover Merlot from the night before. The show was interrupted for a special news bulletin.

"Oh, man, this better be good!" Ted groaned, annoyed that he was missing the show.

The news reporter came on. "Hello, everyone, this just in: Suspected serial killer Ted Bundy escaped from his Colorado jail cell late last night."

"Oh, I've heard of him," Charlie said.

"Ted Bundy is suspected of murdering at least seventeen women in four states," the reporter went on. "He was on trial for a murder in

Colorado, and escaped for the second time last night. He's considered extremely dangerous and could show up just about anywhere. Roadblocks have been set up in Colorado, but he is still on the loose. We'll keep you informed of this case as it progresses; now back to your regular programming."

"We need Sheriff Lobo to catch this guy," Ted said.

"I think this is a bit more serious than Sheriff Lobo," Charlie added.

"I wonder what it must be like to be on the run, having the whole country looking for you?" Ted said.

"I'm sure you'll find out soon enough," Charlie said with a laugh.

Ted threw a sofa pillow at him. "Why makes you think I'd wanna kill someone?" he demanded.

"I don't know."

"I'll admit I've always been interested in criminals; in fact, if I could've gone to college I would've been a criminal psychologist."

"Yeah, that would be a bad-ass job, examining psychos," Charlie said.

"I wish I could've gone to college, but I had to work dead-end jobs instead."

"Oh, son, you didn't go to college because partying was more important to you!" Susan interrupted as she entered the room.

"If you say so, Mom," Ted said, scowling. "First of all, I didn't have a nickel to my name, so how could I go? Second, going to the bar after work for a few beers isn't being a hard core partygoer."

"Oh, look Ted, Lobo just whupped that guy's ass!" Charlie interrupted.

"Oh, yeah, Lobo will get 'em to talk," Ted said as Susan left the room.

"Man, Ted, did you fight with your mom all the time growing up?" Charlie asked.

"No, she just thought everything I did was wrong."

"Well, Ted, I just hope nobody pisses you off, or you'll be in the same cell with Ted Bundy."

"Shut up!"

Chapter 9

Claudia

In late June of 1978, Ted went over to Charlie's house with his second Cadillac.

"Hey, Ted, hot enough for ya?" Charlie said when Ted came to the door.

"Hell yeah, but I still wanna celebrate my cars' being paid off today."

"Finally. Wow, two paid off cars."

"Hell, your Mustang ain't too bad, and it's all paid for."

"Well, what shall we do?" Charlie asked.

"Let's go bowling; the alley up north is doing bowling for burgers."

"What the hell is that?"

"Anyone who bowls over one eighty, gets a free hamburger. Over two hundred get a free cheeseburger, and they make some damn good burgers up there," Ted said.

"Let's go; give me twenty minutes to find my balls and get dressed."

Ted laughed inside at the fact that Charlie said he needed to 'find his balls.' He didn't let Charlie know how immature he was. Ted and Charlie drove separately to the bowling alley. They got a lane without having to wait at all.

"You get warmed up; I'll go get us some beers," Charlie said.

"Great."

They both did poorly on the first game. The second game was better; Charlie won a free hamburger and Ted won a free cheeseburger. They took a little break to eat their food and drink their beers.

"Hey, Teddy, look at the new guys in the lane to our left," Charlie said.

"What about 'em?"

"They think they're King Shit. Wanna bowl em for money, like we used to?"

"You up to it?"

"Hell, yes."

"Okay, I'll go ask 'em."

Ted approached them, swinging his feet as he walked to show cockiness.

"Hey, fellas, you bowl a hell of a ball," Ted said.

"Thanks," they said.

"Ever bowled for money?"

"You think you can beat us?"

"I don't know."

"Okay, but here's the rules. Just me versus you or your partner. No hustling, straight up money game, no bull."

"How much we talking?" Ted asked.

"Fifty dollars."

"Deal," Ted said as he dug out his wallet.

Charlie and Ted decided Ted would play first. They put the money down and the game was on. By the tenth frame, Ted was behind. He only needed a strike and a spare on the tenth to win it. He bowled the first ball, hit the strike. With the second ball he hit seven pins, leaving a six-seven-ten split.

"Come on, Ted, this isn't that hard to pick up," Charlie said.

"Easy for you to say!" Ted grumbled, but bowled the ball the best he could. "Oh, it looks good!" he said while the ball was halfway down the lane.

Unfortunately he only picked up one pin, and lost the game by two pins.

"Good game. Up for another before we leave?" the other guy said.

"No, but it was a good match. Don't spend it all in one place,"

Ted said, as he handed the man fifty dollars.

The other guys packed up and left. As they were leaving, Ted heard the winner ask the others what bar they wanted to go blow the fifty at.

"Great! I could've eaten for a week on that, and they're gonna get plastered with it," Ted said to Charlie.

"I think you did well," the girl in the next lane said suddenly.

"Well, thanks," Ted said with a startled look on his face.

She was beautiful--about 5'7", with long straight blonde hair, a little on the heavy side. Best of all, she was wearing no make-up, but had a naturally pretty face. Her voice was unique and could get anyone to listen. Ted tried to look right in her light-blue eyes when he spoke, but was distracted by this girl's big, round firm chest. She totally caught Ted off-guard.

"Are you staying around?" Ted asked her.

"No, I gotta go; I just practice here for leagues every Friday," she said.

"Oh, well. My name's Ted, by the way. Ted Amichi."

"Claudia Dooley. I'm sorry you lost all your money."

"Oh, well, I didn't lose *all* my money," Ted said, searching for conversation. "Um, a, I, a, well, I make Cadillacs, and I own two."

Charlie watched, trying not to laugh at Ted hitting on the girl.

"Oh, that's nice; I love Cadillacs."

"As I was saying, I have more money, and I would like to buy you a drink. Or take you to dinner. What do you say?"

"That'd be nice, I know just the place," she replied.

"Great, let me just pack up my shit--I mean stuff, pack up my stuff."

"Good going!" Charlie whispered to Ted.

Ted jabbed him in the ribs. "Yeah, yeah. Beat it. I'll meet you at the bar Monday after work, to let you know what happened."

"Okay, don't get your dick caught in your zipper," Charlie said with a laugh.

Ted and Claudia left the alley together. Ted didn't want to take her to some dump like Barney's, so he found a high-class, out of his budget bar to go to. Although he couldn't really afford to come here, he did anyway. After the date, Ted took Claudia home, and she gave him her telephone number.

"See you again sometime, Teddy?" Claudia said.

"Yes, soon."

After work on Monday, Ted was in an exceptionally good mood when he went to the bar to see Charlie and the gang again.

"Well, how'd it go?" Charlie asked.

"It went well; I hope to see her again, ya know," Ted replied.

Ted acted like it was no big deal and he didn't want to talk about it. On the inside, he didn't want to stay long at the bar, because he wanted to get home to call Claudia.

"I'm feeling tired, so I'm going home," Ted said.

"Okay, have fun, I'll probably be leaving soon," Charlie said.

When Ted got home, he didn't even take his shoes off. Instead he raced to the phone to call Claudia. To his surprise she answered on the first ring.

"Hey, Teddy bear, wanna go somewhere?" Claudia said playfully.

"Sure, um, oh boy. Have any ideas?"

"It's your date; tell me what we should do."

"Well, how about we cruise around in my Cadillac? I'll give you a tour of the GM plant."

"Okay, I guess."

"Then we'll go to that fancy doughnut shop for coffee and doughnuts," Ted added.

Ted took a shower and put on some respectable clothes. His wardrobe consisted of very few shirts that weren't ragged and didn't say "Cadillac" on them. If he hadn't been so handsome, his desire to hang out in dump bars and wear ragged clothes wouldn't have worked for him if he were ugly.

That night, Ted took Claudia on a tour of the plant, then to get doughnuts, just as planned. They cruised around the city for a while, in the cool air and empty streets. Claudia rolled down the window and let the air hit her face. Ted felt more relaxed than ever, but wondered if she had the same feeling for him. After a great time, Ted took Claudia back to her place.

"Want me to walk you to the door?" he asked.

"No, thanks, I can handle it," Claudia replied.

"You never know, Ted Bundy might be out here waiting for you."

"Who?"

"Never mind; something I heard on *Sheriff Lobo*."

Although Ted was nice and quite charming, he had a habit of saying stupid things that only he thought were funny. For once he remembered to shut up. He and Claudia put their arms around each other and kissed.

"Come on in, Teddy," Claudia said.

Ted walked in; he noticed her apartment looked nice. His place had dumpster furniture, while her place had the new modern look to it.

That night they slept in the same bed, kissed heavily, but didn't have sex. Ted wanted to, but had a crazy fear that his mother would come out of nowhere and scream at him if he slept around.

One year later, Ted called Charlie with some big news.

"What?" Charlie said.

"That's right, me and Claudia are getting married."

Charlie was sad and happy to hear the news. Sad because Ted wasn't going to be spending much time at the bar anymore, but happy that Ted was getting what he wanted.

"Good job, buddy boy; I don't know what to say," Charlie said.

"I hope to see you at the wedding."

"Of course I'll be there, and I won't crash it, either."

"Oh good, don't do that," Ted said sarcastically.

The wedding was on July 18th. Charlie and his family, Ted's family and Claudia's family were all in the front row. Eighty guests in all showed up. Guys from the bar, the GM plant, as well as guests from Bennigan's, where Claudia worked. The restaurant and catering hall on the outskirts of the city that Ted and Claudia chose made the perfect wedding facility. With a full bar, live band, exotic food service, and a patio with a little outdoor bar, Ted couldn't have asked for more.

Not a drop of rain came from the white fluffy clouds in the sky. Because it was such a warm day, with no wind, Ted and Claudia decided to get married outside on the patio. Ted's white tux, white tie and white shoes didn't have a speck of dirt on them.

Claudia walked up the aisle towards Ted in her long white wedding dress. He stared at her with a cute little grin on his face, feeling like he was in heaven. Even if the sky were falling, he wouldn't have taken his eyes off her. He knew he would never forget this moment. Till the day he died, he thought, he'd always remember this moment. He never planned to get married, but Claudia changed his mind.

"What a great couple we have here!" the minister said just after the vows.

The minister's job is always to say "What a great couple!" This time he meant it; in his mind Ted and Claudia were a modern day Romeo and Juliet. At the reception, Charlie said hi to the newly-married Ted for the first time.

"You look nice for once, Ted," Charlie said.

Claudia walked up to them with a drink in her hand.

"Hello, Mrs. Amichi," Charlie said.

"Hey, Charlie."

"Let's talk later Charlie," Ted said, as he and Claudia headed for the bar.

Charlie talked with the guys Ted worked with at the Cadillac plant.

"Today's a good day to be alive," Charlie said to them.

"Yeah, especially for Ted," one of the guys said.

"Are you sure that's the same Ted Amichi we work with?" one of the GM managers asked.

"Yeah, I know, I've never seen Ted so...so clean, ya know?" another guy said.

"Yeah, usually he's covered in sweat, grease, and Cadillac logo stickers," another said.

Charlie and the guys decorated Ted's Cadillac with wedding decorations and cans on the bumper. At the end of the night, all of them ordered shots. Before they drank Charlie said, "Here's to Ted and Claudia!"

Everyone tipped their glasses and drank. Ted and Claudia were both a little tipsy when the wedding ended. They made their way to the parking lot. Both were relieved to get out of the hot building and into the muggy night air with the stars shining brightly in the sky.

"Oh, my sweet God, what've you done to my car?" Ted groaned.

Everyone laughed and cheered. As Ted and Claudia drove off, everyone chanted, "Teddy and Claudia!" repeatedly.

They headed to their small house in the urban community. Since they were a two-income couple now, the price difference didn't affect them. Ted was more than happy to get rid of his unfavorable apartment in the inner-city ghetto to live in a small house with Claudia. They both knew what they were going to do that night. The fact that they'd waited would make it even more special. This was without a doubt the best day of Ted's life.

Chapter 10

Trouble in the Family

The next morning, the telephone rang bright and early. It was Ted's sister, Mary.

"How did it go yesterday?" Mary asked.

"It went great, but it would've been better if you were there. Why didn't you come to my wedding?" Ted asked.

"Frank wouldn't let me."

"What? That son of a bitch is your husband, not your father."

"Ted..."

"What?"

Mary began to cry, with her voice cracking.

"We just had a baby; I don't want to upset him or he'll hurt the baby. I just can take it when he's mad," Mary said.

"Why don't you let me talk to him? I'll set things right for you."

"Just forget it. I'm so sorry I didn't come yesterday!"

"You don't need to be sorry. But I'm telling you, Frank's gonna end up in a landfill if he doesn't knock it off."

"Please, Ted, just forget it. I gotta go."

"Wait, Mary! Hey, wait," Ted said as Mary hung up the telephone. She was still sobbing and wanted to talk to Ted more, but she was too scared.

"Is your sister okay, honey?" Claudia asked.

"No, she let's that man of hers control her. I know he's a terrible father to that baby."

"That's so sad! How'd she meet him?"

"In high school. I knew him, too. When he got rejected from the football team, he would go to the elementary school to beat up the kids and take their lunch money."

Claudia hugged Ted, her eyes signaling calm sympathy and true love. "Keep a good eye on him," Claudia said.

"If I ever see him on the street, I'm gonna beat up that son of a bitch."

The next day was Monday, time for Ted and Claudia to go to work. Ted was happy to see all the boys at work again. They were all still a bit hung over from the wedding. Ted whistled all day at work, sometimes even sang out loud. Toward the end of the day, a jigsaw almost cut him because he wasn't paying attention.

As time went on, Ted spent less time at the bar with Charlie. He didn't want to lose Charlie as a friend, but being married made him want to lose the whole bar scene. Instead of drinking, he and Charlie got a gym membership. Both agreed to work out three times a week, so they would look and feel better. Ted especially wanted to look good for Claudia.

By Spring 1980, Ted was looking good. He had huge arms, a chest that stuck out, and he weighed well over two hundred pounds. Finally he decided to cut his long hair and dress better.

One night he got a telephone call from Charlie.

"Hey, Ted, have you bought the new 1980 Caddy yet?" Charlie asked.

"No, I'm not doing that anymore; I'm just gonna keep the '77 and the '76."

"Oh, I see marriage has changed you already."

"Yep, and for the better. Besides, the new 80's cars are really made of crap since the gas crunch."

"Yeah, I better not go hot-rodding my Mustang, 'cause these are the last good ones they're gonna make."

"So what's new?" Ted asked.

"Well, now you and I will truly be the same."

"Oh?"

"Yep, remember the girl I met on the construction site? I asked her to marry me and she said yes."

"Oh wow, man, wonderful!"

"She's a good one...beautiful, smart and mine."

"When's the wedding?"

"June 10th at 7:00 P.M., and it's at the same place you got married."

"Good, you know I'll be there."

Ted and Charlie went out that night. They took Ted's '76 Caddy, and had to stop for gas along the way. The Cadillac took twenty-seven gallons to fill; Ted knew he had a long time to wait before it was full. Looking around, he saw his sister Mary at the station. As she turned around, the light reflected off her black eye. Ted didn't notice at first, because he was too busy looking at her swollen, dark red cheeks.

"What happened to you?" Ted asked with sheer anger in his voice.

"It was an accident at work," Mary said firmly.

"Horseshit! Frank did this, huh?"

"Ted, please just forget it. I deserved it."

"How come you're not with him now?"

"He's at Harry's Bar. Just please let it be; I'm not even supposed to be out."

Ted gave Mary a hug. A tear fell on Ted's plaid shirt.

"You tell that son of a bitch to knock it the hell off, and I ain't kidding," Ted said.

"I have to go now."

She got in her car, drove away before Ted could say another thing. Ted tried to chase her down, but decided to stop.

"Whatta ya say we go to Harry's Bar tonight?" Ted asked Charlie.

"Yeah sure, maybe we can say hi to Frankie. You remember Frank from high school?"

"Yeah," Ted said. "At the junior prom, he got arrested for stealing ashtrays from the tables."

After fueling up, they both went to Harry's Bar. Sure enough, they saw Frank. He was easy to spot with his long beard, poorly dyed greasy black hair, 5'5", with a fat belly hanging out of his dirty white tank top.

"I'm gonna get him," Ted said.

"You know if you do anything, he'll take it out on Mary," Charlie said. "I have a better idea."

They waited till Frank came out to the parking lot. Charlie and Ted had put on sunglasses and hats to disguise themselves, then hunched over and started babbling like bums. They approached Frank.

"Hey, dude? Got some spare change, man?" Ted asked.

"Go away! Why the hell you wear sunglasses at night?" Frank asked.

"Come on, dude. Gimme some change, man, or I'll blow ya damn tires out."

"Fuck you!"

Charlie grabbed Frank from behind, put his arms around his neck, holding him while Ted punched him a few times. Frank managed to get a swing in at Ted, right in his eye. Ted shoved Frank up against his own truck. Frank's head hit the driver's window and broke it.

"You son of a bitch!" Frank yelled.

Ted was ready to take off, but Charlie stopped him.

"Wait, take his wallet, so it looks like he was mugged," Charlie whispered.

Ted twisted Frank's arm while Charlie took his wallet.

"All I wanted was some spare change, dude. Now I got your whole wallet," Ted said to Frank in a sloppy voice.

"You goddamn derelicts. If I ever catch you, I'm gonna rip your fucking heads off!" Frank wheezed.

Ted and Charlie walked away. Frank tried to get up, but his fat, dirty drunken ass just couldn't.

"You fuckheads," Frank continued weakly.

Ted and Charlie were far away, over in the shadows where they'd hidden the Caddy, but they could still hear Frank cursing up a storm.

"That'll learn him," Ted said, grinning.

"Oh, no!" Charlie said in a panic.

"What?"

"You got a black eye. How are you gonna explain that to Claudia?"

"We'll see," Ted said, not bothered by it. "I'm sure I'll think of something."

After a few drinks at their own bar, Ted took Charlie home.

"I'll see you at your wedding, Charlie," Ted said.

"Okay, have a good one."

Ted turned off all the lights in the house as he entered. He went right to the bed, tiptoeing around to make as little noise as possible.

"Teddy, what's wrong?" Claudia asked.

"Nothing, just tired," Ted said in a quiet voice.

Claudia turned on the bedroom lamp and gasped when she saw Ted's eye.

"Oh, my! What happened to your face?"

Ted was desperately trying to think of a story. He knew he needed to think of something good, but if he took too long to answer, it would still look bad.

"Well, at the bar, um, a...a guy had a flat tire, and needed help. So, I, then, ya know, a, helped he and the bolts on his tires were rusted shut. So, um, ya know, we both gave the lugwrench a lot of force. It slipped when the bolt came loose, and hit me in the eye," Ted said with an innocent smile on his face.

"Yeah, right," Claudia said sarcastically. "I was born at night, but not last night."

"It'll heal; I was just glad to help someone. Ya know, do a good deed."

Claudia stared him down with her loving, yet dead serious blue eyes. Ted folded like an umbrella.

"What really happened? You're lying," Claudia said in a strict voice.

"Well, um, only half lying; I really did do a good deed for someone, but, well, ya know."

"Tell me...now!" Claudia repeated.

"All right, all right. Frank beat Mary up again. I mean real bad. So me and Charlie dressed up like bums and beat him up and mugged him. But he got one shot in the dark at me."

Claudia nodded her head and hugged Ted. He was surprised she didn't start screaming from all sides at him.

"Don't lie to me again, Teddy," she said.

"Okay, sure, no problem."

"Also, don't ever beat up Frank again, even though he deserves it."

"You got it," Ted said in a relieved voice.

They both hugged again, and Claudia shut off the bedroom light. Ted was still surprised at how well she had taken it. He grinned to himself, thinking of Frank.

On Charlie's wedding day, Ted wanted to do anything and everything in his power to make it as much fun as Charlie had made his wedding. Ted and the boys even decorated Charlie's car. After the wedding, Ted and Claudia went out to dinner at Michigan Steakhouse.

"I'm glad to see that Charlie's getting what he wants," Claudia said.

"Yeah, I knew it'd only be a matter of time," Ted replied.

"I remember he looked kinda sad after our wedding."

"I hope his marriage is as happy as ours has been."

"Yeah, we were meant for each other, but we still don't have one thing," Claudia said.

"Yeah, I know, a sports car."

"No! A child, Ted."

This surprised him. "You want to have a kid?"

"I can't have kids for some reason, but I want one."

"Wow, Claudia, how come you never told me this?"

"I just found out recently that I can't, but I still want a child."

"Well, I guess if that's what you want, but I'm not sure where they're giving away kids."

"Adoption maybe?" Claudia suggested.

"Okay, sure, whatever."

"Damn it, Ted, I'm serious; we should go to an adoption agency and check it out."

Ted's body shook at the thought of adoption, at taking in some stranger's child. Why couldn't she just forget this whole thing? He thought.

"Um, well, we'll see what happens, but I don't like adoption agencies," Ted replied.

"Oh, all right, forget it!" Claudia said in an angry voice.

When they got home after a nice meal, Ted went right to the phone to call Charlie. He hid in the bedroom where Claudia would not hear his conversation.

"Congrats on your new marriage Charlie," Ted said.

"Thanks, man," Charlie replied.

"Hey, I hate to bug you on your wedding night, but I need to talk."

"Sure. What's up, man?"

"Claudia just told me she wants to adopt a kid."

"So?"

"If we go to an adoption agency, my little secret will come out."

"Oh, yeah," Charlie said seriously. "Claudia doesn't know about that, huh?"

"No, and I want to keep it that way."

"Well, Ted, I think you should come clean. It's the only solution. Anyway, I'm gonna go now. I got some things to do, ya know?"

"Yeah, all right; have fun tonight, Charlie."

"Oh, you better believe I will!"

Chapter 11

Breaking the News

Ted's secret would remain a secret until his fourth wedding anniversary in 1983.

Ted and Claudia were sitting up in bed watching late-night television when the telephone rang.

"Hello," Ted said.

"Hello, Mr. Amichi? This is Detroit City Hospital," the voice said.

"What is it?"

"We're calling to inform you that your sister Mary has been in a car crash."

"Oh, my God. How bad?"

"She was killed instantly; the other driver was drunk."

Ted sat in silence; he didn't want to believe it was true.

"I'm so sorry, sir," the voice said.

Ted hung up the telephone. Claudia overheard, so she gave him comfort. He didn't get much sleep that night. It seemed every couple of hours he would wake up hoping it was a bad dream, but reality shot him down each time.

At the funeral, Ted comforted his crying mother. Mary's son, Tommy, was four years old and in the worst situation ever -- no mother, and having Frank for a father. Ted noticed Frank talking to his bar buddies. Ted walked closer and could hear what was being said.

"Oh, shit, I'm gonna have to find another bitch to cook for me now," Frank said to his bar buddies.

Ted was headed toward Frank with his fists clenched. Claudia grabbed him and turned him around.

"Don't do it; not here," Claudia said.

After the funeral, Ted and Claudia saw little Tommy, who was still crying, with Frank, who wasn't crying at all.

"Hey, shut the hell up, kid!" Frank said as he shoved Tommy into the car.

Ted felt a puking sensation coming on, because he knew there wasn't a thing that he could do.

"I was right; Frank didn't care for Mary at all," Ted said to Claudia.

"Yeah, no kidding," she replied.

Ted didn't want to flatter himself that he was right. He just wanted Mary back and wished she could have been happier before she died. Ted and Claudia didn't say another word till they were in the car driving home.

"You know, Tommy's the real victim here," Claudia said.

"We need to do something," Ted replied.

"You know, if we can prove child abuse, maybe we could adopt Tommy."

"It's true. He's family, and a great kid."

"Oh, yeah, I'd love to have Tommy."

"If we don't do something, with Frank for a father, Tommy's likely to become the next Ted Bundy."

"Who's this Ted Bundy you always mention?" Claudia asked.

"Never mind; I just wish we could adopt him," Ted said with sorrow.

"Why don't we call a lawyer? I bet we can get custody of him. We could have a child like we wanted, and be doing something good for the world," Claudia said.

"Yeah, and ourselves. I mean, this kid is my flesh and blood, and you saw how Frank treats him."

"I know; you don't tell a kid to shut up when his mother just died."

When they got home it didn't take long for them to go to sleep. The next morning Claudia called a lawyer she knew who came into her restaurant often. At work, Ted was struggling. He couldn't get his mind off how Frank had treated Tommy.

"I owe it to my sister, and Tommy, and Claudia and me," Ted said to himself.

Ted knew the secret from his past had to come out eventually. He was worried about what Claudia would think of him. That night, when he came home, he saw Claudia glowing with happiness. This worried him, because he sure wasn't glowing with happiness.

"Guess what, Ted? The lawyer did a background check on Frank and found out he has six DUI's and drug charges. Also we can be witnesses to his abuse yesterday."

"Wow, this is, um, great!" Ted said with a crack in his voice.

"Yes, he said maybe within a month or two we could have custody."

"I don't know."

"All right, there is something else too," Claudia said.

"What do you mean?"

"Well, it's gonna cost lots of money, but surely that's okay with you?"

"Well, maybe we could just find another way."

"What are you saying? The money should be the least of it! With our jobs we can cover it, honey."

"I don't care about the money; Tommy's worth it. But, well, why don't we just have Frank killed?" Ted said sarcastically.

"What? Shut up! Don't even joke about things like that. I made an appointment with the lawyer for tomorrow. He said we need to discuss the court process. He really wants to get going soon."

"Well, look, let's just talk to Frank. Maybe see if he'll just give Tommy up without a fight in court," Ted said.

"All right, fine!" Claudia said in an angry tone.

Ted breathed in relief that he didn't have to tell his secret. He knew it wouldn't stay quiet forever, though, and he was right; less than a week later it came up again.

"Ted, the lawyer talked to Frank. Frank said there is no way in hell he's giving up Tommy," Claudia said.

"Goddamn it!" Ted scowled.

"What's wrong with you, honey?"

"We can't get him if Frank won't give him up."

"We don't need Frank; the lawyer said it will be a cinch to get custody. Frank is a convicted alcohol offender, and he's unemployed; it'll be easy to prove he's unfit. Besides, we're family."

"Well, um, yeah, but, I, oh man!"

"What! Don't you want a child?" Claudia said louder than normal.

"Yes, I do."

"If it's the money, we can cover it. I'll do whatever it takes," she said, almost pleading.

"It's not the fucking money," Ted growled.

Claudia saw that Ted was looking sad and noticed his hand shaking. Ted very rarely cursed at her. She knew something was terribly wrong. She put her hand in his hand and felt that he was cold as ice.

"What is it, then?" she asked.

Ted knew he had to come clean. This was it; no way out. He wondered if he should have Charlie here to help. After thinking about it for a minute, he decided that was stupid; he could handle it himself. He took a deep breath and looked Claudia right in the eyes.

"Claudia, honey, when I was eighteen, I got convicted of felony assault. I'm a felon; that'll prevent a judge from awarding custody to us," Ted said in a trembling voice.

"Oh, my God! What'd you do?" she asked supportively.

"It's a long story, and I would rather discuss it with the lawyer."

"Okay."

Ted was relieved, but still unsure if he'd done the right thing. He'd been hoping to take the secret with him to the grave. But the next morning he and Claudia went to see the lawyer.

"The background check on you Ted, shows a felony conviction. I want you to tell me what happened," the lawyer said.

"If I do, can we still get custody of Tommy?" Ted asked.

"If you don't, you'll never get custody. Without total honesty, maybe at least someone else can," the lawyer said.

"No, not someone else; we want him! We'll love and cherish

him," Claudia said with tears in her eyes.

"Tell me what happened, Ted," the lawyer said.

"I was found guilty, even though I was innocent."

"Uh-huh, I see, that's good. If we could dig up the case and go back to court, maybe we can get a retrial."

"Really?"

"Yes, and if we win, then getting custody of Tommy will be easy. There probably won't even be much of a trial."

"So the big thing here is getting my conviction overturned?" Ted asked.

"Yes."

Ted smiled and was somewhat relieved. He knew he really was innocent. "Oh God, I've been wanting to get it off my record for so long. I was innocent; it was self-defense. Being a felon sucks."

"Explain what happened," the lawyer prompted him. "Names and dates, so I can research."

"Okay, it was May 18,1968 when I got arrested. I was accused of beating up a teacher in high school. I got school credits for being his student aid, and he paid me for my work I did."

"Go on."

Claudia looked at Ted with sadness in her eyes. She didn't know whether to feel bad for him, or be mad at him. She was anxious to hear the story, hanging on every word.

"I used to do everything for him. He gave me money to buy him coffee every morning. He would always give me extra to buy myself something. I graded his papers and organized his desk. I noticed he was giving me much more money then I really deserved. Well, me being young, I just enjoyed it and didn't think of why he was doing it. On that particular day, he said he wanted me to stay after school and help him with something. He promised me five dollars if I stayed a few hours. I did and after everyone was out of the classroom, it happened."

"What happened?" the lawyer asked.

"The man put his hands on me. He smiled, and said I owed it to him, for what he'd done for me. At that point, I punched him in the face and he fell to the ground. He got up and hit me back. In the end,

I shoved him though a classroom window. In court, I had no chance, because he was a respected teacher, and I was just a kid. My public defender was an imbecile; I would've done better defending myself. I was found guilty and sentenced to two hundred hours' community service and ten days in the hole. I had to go to another school to graduate."

"What was the teacher's name?"

"Kipler, Jeff Kipler."

"Have you seen him since?"

"Nope, not for over fourteen years," Ted said.

"Well, let me do some research; tomorrow I'll tell you what we can do."

Ted and Claudia left in a hurry.

"Wow, Ted, how come you never told me this?" Claudia asked.

"Oh, come on, why do you think?"

"I understand," Claudia said.

"Well, I guess I screwed our chances of any adoption."

"Let's just wait; maybe this lawyer can get you a retrial."

Ted and Claudia hugged and went home. That night, while Claudia was in the shower, for the first time since he was a kid, Ted prayed.

"Dear God, I really need help. I want Tommy to be my adopted son, and the only way is to get my conviction overturned. You know what happened. Please help me, please," Ted said in a desperate voice.

"Who were you talking to, honey?" Claudia said as she came out of the shower.

"Nobody; let's just go to bed."

Ted slept well and peacefully, even though he had so much to think about.

Chapter 12

Getting Everything I Want

Four days later, Monday morning at 7:00 A.M., the telephone rang. Ted was asleep and didn't want to answer it.

"Who the hell could that be this early?" Ted mumbled at the phone.

Claudia answered it, because she didn't want Ted to have to get up.

"Ted, it's our lawyer; he wants to talk to you."

"Hello," Ted said.

"Hello, Mr. Amichi. I've got some good news. I looked up Jeff Kipler. I couldn't find an address, because he's in the Michigan State Penitentiary for six counts of child molestation involving a Boy Scout troop in 1977."

Ted suddenly went from dead tired to lively and awake.

"Oh, my God! Does that mean I'm off the hook?"

"I'd say so, but don't celebrate yet; it's not 100% sure."

"Hell no, but it sure helps."

The lawyer quoted Ted a fee of $4,000 for his services, for both filing for the retrial, and proceeding with the adoption. They both hung up, and Ted told Claudia the good news.

"I know, I was on the extension," she said, hugging him. "I knew you were innocent, I can't believe they would let someone like this Kipler be a teacher, and a Boy Scout leader."

On Tuesday, Ted went to Tommy's school, to see how he was doing. He saw Tommy walking home from kindergarten.

"Hey, kid, how you holding up?" Ted asked.

"Okay," Tommy replied.

Ted noticed two black eyes, and that the kid seemed really sad. He was a cute kid, with his straight black hair and big brown puppy-dog eyes.

"What happened to your face?" Ted asked.

"I got hurt at school." He sounded just the way his mother had when she made excuses.

"How would you like to live with me and Claudia?"

Tommy looked up, Ted saw a bit of happiness in his face. It looked as if Tommy was going said yes, but instead he looked behind him, saw Frank's truck, and began to walk fast.

"I have to go; 'bye."

Ted started his car and tried to chase him down. As Ted drove faster, Tommy ran faster to get away.

"Wait -- oh, damn it!" Ted said as he saw Tommy running towards Frank's truck.

Ted went home. He didn't even say hi to Claudia; instead he got the phone and called Frank.

"Yeah?" Frank said when he answered the phone.

"Oh, is that how you answer your phone?" Ted asked.

"What do you want, Ted?"

"Why is Tommy beat up?"

"He got hurt at school. Why? Did the little bastard tell you I beat him up?"

"No, but it sure is funny, Mary and Tommy always had accidents."

"Screw you, you old busy-body."

"What!"

"Why are you calling me, mother-fucker?"

"Mother-fucker, yeah, that's your answer to everything, just scream obscenities!" Ted yelled. "Right, Frank, isn't that what you do when I got you cornered?"

"What do you want, Ted?"

"Stop hitting Tommy, okay?"

"Oh yeah, I'll do that! Hey, Tommy, get yer ass over here."

Ted heard a smack! and crying from Tommy, along with laughter coming from Frank.

"Hey, Frank, why don't you come over here and hit me?" Ted said.

Frank hung up without saying goodbye.

"Don't piss Frank off; he'll just take it out on Tommy," Claudia said when Ted hung up.

"He needs to be stood up to. Mary and Tommy never said a damn word to him. That's why he thinks it's okay to do these things," Ted protested.

"You're not going to get through to Frank. He's a thug. Let's just get Tommy through the lawyer."

The next day the lawyer called Ted again.

"Well, Ted, we did it. The D.A. made Mr. Kipler an offer. Since he is up for parole in ten months, they said if he told the truth about what happened between you and him in 1968, not only would he not be charged for what happened, but it would make a huge impact on his parole hearing."

"Did it work?"

"Yes, and your stories matched. He said he took the deal because he wanted to get out. Prison life has been unbearable for him."

"Hold on, let me wipe away a tear here," Ted said in a sarcastic voice.

The lawyer and Ted laughed a little.

"What next?" Ted asked.

"Well, the D.A. doesn't want a retrial, but in two weeks you must appear in court, they'll dismiss the charges and expunge your record."

"Great. How soon can we start the adoption process?"

"Not till this is completely cleared up. Then we can start on the custody battle."

"I saw Tommy yesterday; he had two black eyes. Every day that goes by he's getting more and more abused by Frank."

"I know, but we'll just have to wait this through. But we've gotten the big step out of the way. Now it's just a matter of time."

"Thank you so much."

"No problem. You'll get my bill in the mail. I've already started the research for the custody battle. I did some more research on Frank, and for no extra charge I'll give you a surprise at the custody trial."

"What's the surprise?"

"You'll see."

"Okay, you'll get your money before the end of the week; once again, thank you."

Ted sold his '77 Cadillac to an old lady down the street. She'd always commented on how plush his Caddy was when he drove by her house every morning. He'd always thought she was annoying. She talked his ear off every morning, and sometimes caused him to be late because she won't stop talking. For once he was glad he'd met her, because she gave him four thousand one hundred dollars for the car.

"Why didn't you just sell your old '76 Cadillac, honey?" Claudia asked.

"I can't; it's special to me, since it was my first. Besides, I couldn't get enough for it."

Ted went to his court appearance. Finally, after fourteen years, his past conviction was dropped. He paid off the lawyer completely. It took six months before the custody trial day came. As the lawyer said, winning was easy as could be. After hours of a lot of boring paperwork, Ted and Claudia became Tommy's legal parents. Even Tommy's name was changed to Thomas Amichi.

"Ready for your surprise, Ted?" the lawyer said as they were on their way out of court.

"Yeah."

Frank brushed past them, scowling at Claudia. The lawyer and Ted looked at him. After having to sign the final document to give up Tommy, Frank had thrown the pen on the desk and stormed toward the door.

"Screw this shit, I'm getting drunk!" Frank said to himself as he was almost out the door.

The lawyer looked at Ted and Claudia with a smile. Two cops stopped Frank just before he could open the door, to leave the courtroom.

"Frank Miller, you're under arrest," one cop said.

"What! For what?"

"You've got an outstanding drug warrant from a few years back. We got an anonymous tip that you would be here today," the cop said as he cuffed Frank.

"Fuck!"

Frank's loud voice echoed throughout the whole courthouse.

Ted, Tommy and Claudia left the courthouse, skipping and giggling as they walked to the car. They saw Frank bawling his eyes out in the back of the police car outside the courthouse.

"Well, we did it," Claudia said when they all came home together for the first time.

"Yep, it worked," Ted replied.

Claudia showed Tommy his new bedroom. Ted and Claudia had it all ready with toys and a Star Wars bedspread on the bed.

"And as soon as you unpack your stuff, come out in the kitchen and we'll have cake!" Claudia promised him. While Tommy's unpacking, she wanted to talk with Ted alone.

"I'm so sorry you had to sell your '77 Cadillac to pay for all this," Claudia said.

"Hell, I'm not," Ted said with a smile.

"Really?"

"Think about it, I helped my dead sister and Tommy. Also, I finally got rid of the horrible secret from my past. If you only knew how many years it's been bugging me. It almost prevented me from getting the job at GM. Heck, the Cadillac's just a car, but I'm feeling great."

"I'm so glad to hear that," Claudia said as she hugged Ted.

"Also, I'm due for a raise this summer. I'm thinking of buying a brand-new car next year. I want it completely loaded with options. Not only am I not mad, I wanna celebrate."

"Hmm, I bet you wanna go out cruising and drinking with Charlie, huh?"

"Oh, I don't have to; it's Friday, we can go do something together."

"It's okay, for a few hours. Just remember tomorrow night is our night," Claudia said in a happy voice.

"Yes sir, tomorrow night is our night," Ted said joyfully.

"'Sir'? What the hell is that all about?"

They both laughed while Ted got dressed.

"Oh, remember, don't get drunk, and no fights," Claudia said to Ted as he was leaving.

"Yeah, yeah."

Chapter 13

Feeling Good

Ted got the raise at work that summer. By Thanksgiving 1984 he'd saved up enough money to buy a brand-new car with cash. Tommy was growing up nicely and starting to forget all about Frank. The night before Thanksgiving, the GM plant threw a turkey party for the employees from 7:00 to 9:00 P.M. Ted showed up at 7:30 with Charlie, Claudia and little Tommy. They ate at the buffet and drank sparkling cider. The DJ came in with some tunes. Within minutes Ted and Claudia were dancing away. Towards the end of the night, one of the employees who worked with Ted brought him a wishbone.

"Make a wish, Mr. Amichi," he said.

"What are you gonna wish for, Ted?" others yelled.

Ted stood there pondering. Finally it hit him what to say.

"Well, Ted, what's it gonna be?" Charlie asked.

Everyone was staring at him waiting for a reply. Ted intentionally took a while, because he liked the fact that everyone wondered what he wanted. A few years ago, nobody knew or cared about him. Now everyone liked him.

"You wanna know what I want?" Ted said.

"What? A flying Cadillac?" one of them said.

They all laughed; Ted thought a flying Cadillac might be fun, but it wasn't what he wanted.

"No, that's not it," Ted replied.

"What then?"

"Nothing, absolutely nothing at all. I have everything I want, and everyone I want. I couldn't ask for anything more."

All of them stood there in surprise. They hadn't expected such a deep answer. They'd thought Ted would say something goofy like "a flying Cadillac" or "a boob job for Claudia" or "an endless supply of beer." Claudia came up and put her arm around him. He pulled the wishbone and got the bigger half.

The next year he got promoted from plant worker to sales. Now he wasn't always dirty and sweaty, but instead clean and cunning. Ted didn't stop there; he kept advancing with his home life as well. In 1989, Ted and Claudia sold their house in the urban community they'd lived in for ten years, and bought a big new house in the suburbs. The only drawback was, once they moved to a different area, Ted didn't spend much time with Charlie anymore.

On Ted's 16th wedding anniversary in 1995, he decided to take Claudia on a second honeymoon to Las Vegas. Tommy was almost sixteen, doing well in school, had a job, a girlfriend, and a new GM car. Using Ted's discount benefits helped him a lot. Tommy was one of the very few kids in his school to have a brand-new car. Ted and Claudia were headed out the door to the airport, when Ted remembered to give Tommy some parting advice.

"No parties or strippers while we're gone, you hear?" Ted said to Tommy.

"Oh, I know, I know."

Ted hoped Tommy wasn't serious about not having parties or girls, because he remembered every time his mother left him alone for a while--it was party-time.

When Ted and Claudia got to their hotel room in Vegas, they were too tired to do anything, so they went to bed.

"Would you marry me again?" Ted asked Claudia.

"I would marry you a million times. Are you happy with me?" Claudia asked Ted.

"I'm happy in general; I'm on top of the world and you are my queen."

When Claudia got up to go to the bathroom, Ted opened the window, letting the hot, muggy, night breeze flow across his face. The view from the tenth floor blew him away. So many lights, and only distant Frank Sinatra music could be heard. Ted put his hands together and made a prayer.

"Dear God, you've been good to me. I'm happy as can be. So, I tell you what, please keep everything just they way it is, and I will be the best person I can be, to anyone. I'll even stop making fun of the retarded employee at work. I thank you for such a good life; I couldn't ask for anything more. I am truly a lucky man," Ted smiled and said Amen.

"Who were you talking to, Teddy?" Claudia asked, coming out of the bathroom.

"Um, just talking to myself."

"Out loud?" Claudia wondered.

"Yes," Ted said with an innocent smile on his face.

"I think the desert heat has fried your brains," Claudia said as she laughed.

They laughed, kissed and went back to bed. Ted felt embarrassed to talk out loud to God in front of Claudia. He and Claudia had never picked a religion, or gone to church. Ted felt strange making prayers, because he felt he should be a better Christian.

Ted was ready to start thinking about retirement within the next ten to fifteen years. He and Claudia had both saved up a lot money with Ted's good job. Their new house was almost paid off. Claudia's car, Ted's new car, and the good old 1976 Cadillac was paid off. By Ted's 46th birthday in 1999, Tommy had moved out of his parents' house and in with his girlfriend, but he came over to see Ted on his birthday. He even helped Claudia decorate the cake.

"How come you didn't invite Charlie over?" Claudia asked.

"I should; it's been almost two years since I've seen him."

"Do you not like Charlie anymore?"

"I do, it's just that we're both so busy with our own families, that, well, you know."

Ted and Claudia had been married twenty years. As Ted blew out the candles on the cake, he thought he was doing all right.

Chapter 14

Counselor

It was February 1999, just three weeks after Ted's birthday. Ted and Claudia were watching TV. A commercial came on that caught Claudia's eye.

"Hello, I'm Ann Ritz, and I'm a licensed marriage and family counselor. I'm interested in giving your marriage the boost it needs. For a low fee, I can help marriages barely hanging by a thread, or those just in need of a tune up. I can help you spice up your love life. Even if you're a happy couple, I can make you happier. Marriages, like cars, sometimes need routine maintenance. So come see me, Ann Ritz, today, in the Detroit downtown center. Or call me at; 555-9897."

Ted eyed this woman suspiciously. She was in her forties, with long brown hair, green eyes, a bit overweight. To him she seemed a little butch, a little too aggressive. Even though it was just a commercial, it made Ted feel twitchy and he didn't know why.

"Oh Ted, can we go see her?" Claudia asked.

"What? You think our marriage is in trouble?" Ted was surprised.

"Oh, not really."

"Why then?"

"Oh it'll be fun; I've heard these marriage counselors can spice up our love and make our marriage even better."

"You really want to? I wouldn't trust that one. She looks like a classic bitch."

"Well, now that our little Tommy's moved out, we need to try something exciting. Besides, I've always wondered what those counselors are like; it might be fun just to see. I just, I don't know, feel bored," Claudia replied.

"I don't know; there's just something about her I don't like."

"Is it the money?"

"Oh, hell, no, you're worth anything to me. It's just, counselors are too--well, I don't know; I just don't like them."

"Please, Ted, please," Claudia begged.

Ted really didn't want to; the sight of that woman made him want to puke. But he'd do anything for Claudia.

"Oh, all right, whatever, schedule us an appointment. How bad can it be?"

"Oh boy!" Claudia said as she reached for the telephone.

Ann Ritz was so busy with clients, it took over three weeks to get an appointment. Finally the day came. Ted and Claudia drove into town in the old '76 Cadillac, which Ted still kept up and running after all these years.

"Welcome, Ted and Claudia," Ann said with a smile, leading them into her office.

Ted was hoping the roof would cave in so they could leave. Ann Ritz was even worse in real life than in the commercial. In his mind she was old and overweight, yet she still wore a tight, revealing dress. Her bleach blond hair had phony red highlights and was poorly curled and parted in the middle. Ted couldn't help but to look at her chest; she wasn't wearing a bra, and her breasts sagged like over-ripe fruit. Her hard-looking face reminded him of one of the guys he worked with. As she turned around to lead them into her office, he noticed flowers in her hair. Ted rolled his eyes when he saw that this counselor had an acoustic guitar by her desk.

"So, Claudia, how's Ted treating you?" Ann asked as they all sat down.

"Oh, really great."

"Explain 'great.' What does he do?"

"Well, we always go out on Saturdays. I see him all the time during the week. Oh, except for Fridays."

"Why not Fridays?" Ann asked suspiciously.

"Friday's his night to go out drinking with the boys."

Ted smiled, even though he was pissed off that Ann hadn't asked him how Claudia treated him. Ann eyed Ted like he was something under a microscope.

"Ted's wonderful," Claudia went on. "We went on a second honeymoon three years ago. We never fight and he'll do anything to please me or our adopted son Tommy. I couldn't be happier. We are just a little bored and need something new and fun," she added.

"Ted, would you leave the room?' Ann said abruptly.

"Why?" The request startled him.

"Just do it, please. It's part of the process."

"Don't tell me what to do without telling me why," he said, more than a little annoyed.

"Ted, it's obvious to me that you already completely control your wife, but don't try to control me," Ann said.

"I don't control my wife," Ted said defensively.

"Ted, please. This is hard enough on Claudia. That's a great story you made her tell, but it's not believable. What did you threaten to do to her if she told the truth?" Ann asked.

"Oh, Ted, just do as she says, for me," Claudia said, signaling with her eyes that she wanted to get it over with.

Ted left just so he wouldn't embarrass Claudia. He slammed the door behind him. With Ted gone, Ann and Claudia spoke more.

"Really, Ted doesn't control me; he's the best," Claudia said.

"Honey, he does; you just don't know it," Ann said as she put her hand out to Claudia.

"No." Claudia shook her head.

"Come on, he went out drinking on Friday. You know he's cheating on you; don't deny it to yourself."

"No!" Claudia insisted.

"Claudia, let me tell you the facts of life. Any man who goes out that much and won't even let me have a word alone with you is completely controlling. I'll bet he wouldn't even let you come here without a fight."

"Well...I did have to beg him, but he finally said it was okay."

"Beg? You're a grown woman; you don't have to beg anyone.

You don't need him."

Ted came barging in; he'd been listening in on them the whole time.

"Are you done bad-mouthing me to my wife?" Ted asked.

"Ted, get out of here!" Claudia said, angered.

Ted was surprised that she was angry, so he left. He didn't want to make a scene, but this counselor was going too far, in his opinion.

"You see?" Ann asked. "You can even be here for five minutes without him having to be here. When was the last time you had fun?"

"Me and Teddy always go out. We even went to Las Vegas on a second honeymoon three years ago."

"No, no, I mean you. Not you and Ted, just you. When was the last time you had fun alone?"

"I don't go out alone; I love to go with Ted."

"Oh, I see. He can go out drinking with the boys without you, but you can't go out without him."

"Well, um, I guess."

"Take my word for it; you're being controlled by him and don't even know it. I can help you."

"I don't feel that way," Claudia insisted.

"Trust me; you are. I'd like you to come and see me privately this time next Tuesday."

"Ted won't like that."

"You don't need Ted's permission. You can request time off from work and come see me every Tuesday. I'd also like to prescribe some medication for you."

"What is it?"

"Something that will relax you and help you think better and more clearly."

"How much is this stuff gonna cost?" Claudia asked.

"Ted works for GM, doesn't he? Your health insurance should cover it."

Claudia hesitated. "But I wouldn't want Ted to know I was taking pills."

"See, you are afraid of Ted. You have to learn to stand up for yourself."

Claudia was in a state of shock from what Ann was saying. Until now she'd thought she was happy in life. However, she'd always been intimidated by someone with a college degree and a high-paying job, like Ann.

One secret she'd never told Ted was that when they were adopting Tommy, if the lawyer had told her to jump, she would have said "How high?" She was so insecure when the lawyer came into her restaurant in a thousand dollar suit, and she stood there wearing her Bennigan's waitress outfit, that she'd almost been afraid to talk to him, even though rescuing Tommy had been the most important thing in her life back then.

It was that same insecurity that made her take the prescription from Ann, even though she didn't want to. Ann went outside to bring Ted back in.

"Are you done?" he asked Ann, not even pretending to keep the hostility out of his voice. His tone toward Claudia was softer. "Come on honey, let's go."

"She doesn't have to go until she's ready," Ann said.

"I'm ready," Claudia said.

"Or you're just scared to say no to him," Ann said as Claudia stood up. "Don't forget what we talked about," she added, meaning their appointment the following Tuesday.

Ted didn't ask what Ann meant. He just wanted to get out of there.

"Wow, did that suck," he said when they got to the car.

"If you say so," Claudia said in a frustrated voice.

On the way home Claudia was in a daze, thinking about what Ann had said. Later, when Ted was watching TV after dinner, she took the car and went to the supermarket, stopping at the pharmacy to fill the prescription Ann had given her.

That night, Claudia spent a long time alone in the bathroom, thinking and looking at the pills. She could hear Ann's voice, as if she was right in the room with her. To stop Ann's voice in her head, she took one of the pills, and went to bed, where Ted was still watching TV. He shut it off when she got into bed. Usually they were all over each other, but that night they didn't even speak.

By the time Tuesday came, Claudia had been on the pills for a week. She told her boss she had a doctor's appointment, and took time off from work to go to Ann's office.

"So, did you have to sneak away? Or did you tell Ted you were coming?" Ann greeted.

"I snuck away," Claudia admitted.

"Are the pills helping?"

"They seem to be helping," Claudia said. "I've been really cheery lately."

"I want you to work on your assertiveness this week," Ann instructed her. "You pick something and tell Ted 'no.' It will help you regain your self-esteem."

"What should I say no to?"

"Anything, you want, but sex would be a start. And I'll give you another prescription to refill those pills."

Ann charged a hundred dollars per session. Instead of charging it to Ted's health insurance, Claudia snuck the money out of the joint bank account so Ted wouldn't know about the secret meetings. The pills made her feel high and giggly. Ted loved to see her so happy, but wondered why. He knew it wasn't a heartfelt happy, but more like a drug addict happy. And he wondered why Claudia didn't seem interested in sex lately. Four weeks after that first session with the marriage counselor, Ted was disturbed. Claudia lay in bed one night laughing much too hard at what was on TV.

"Ever since we saw that phony marriage counselor you've been acting weird," Ted said. "Are you okay?"

"Yeah sure, blame it on her! Can't I be happy without you trying to fucking control me?"

Ted knew something was up; Claudia never cursed like that. Ted hadn't heard such dirty sloppy talk since he used to go to the bar every night. He stood over the bed, horrified to hear his neat, suburban daisy wife act like some drunken thug.

"Do you wanna, ya know, have fun tonight? It's been a while," Ted said.

"No, just let me go to bed," Claudia said.

She wouldn't say another word. Ted was regretting more and

more agreeing to see the counselor; he couldn't help thinking she was to blame.

After six weeks, Claudia had spent over one thousand dollars between the pills and her secret counseling sessions. Ted noticed the withdrawals from the bank account. The mortgage was going to have to be mailed late. Claudia's paychecks were getting smaller each week. Since she was paid hourly, it only meant she was ditching work. When Claudia came home from work, or wherever she'd been, Ted approached her.

"Where's the money going?" Ted asked her, almost afraid of the answer. He was sickened to see that her eyes were bloodshot and her face was pale.

"How should I know?" Claudia screamed. "Quit blaming me for everything!"

"I just asked if you knew where the money is."

Claudia went into a violent rage, hitting Ted several times and screaming horrible obscenities. Ted grabbed her arms and restrained her.

"Let me go, you son of a bitch! I hate you!" she yelled.

Ted let her go; he couldn't believe his darling wife, whom he'd spent most of his life with, was going crazy and he couldn't stop it. When she said she hated him, it hit Ted harder than anyone ever could. Claudia began to cry as she ran out the door.

"Wait! What's wrong? This is crazy!" Ted said.

She kept running and didn't stop till she was in her car. She drove away, leaving skid marks in the driveway. Ted went upstairs to the bedroom to begin looking through Claudia's stuff. He found the pills and an appointment book. The book showed every time Claudia had seen Ann Ritz, and how many pills she'd taken.

"I guess this is where the thousand dollars went. I knew Ann Ritz was responsible for this," Ted said to himself.

He knew he couldn't just let Claudia go. Determined not to let Ann Ritz ruin Claudia, he took the pills and put them in his pocket. He wondered if he should take one himself, to see their effect. He decided not to; he needed to keep his head clear.

Claudia didn't come home till midnight. She took a pill from an extra bottle she had in her purse, and slept on the sofa, not even saying hi to Ted.

The next morning Ted got up early. Bags under his eyes were visible from lack of sleep. He took the pills to the local hospital to ask if someone could tell him what they were. A clerk told him the pharmacist would call him back sometime that afternoon.

At work, his cunning hardworking voice just couldn't sell anything. He yelled at an employee who was being difficult. His fifteen-minute breaks turned into thirty-minute breaks. He went back to the hospital after work, to talk with the pharmacist instead of waiting for his call.

"So what are these pills?' Ted asked.

"They're a powerful antidepressant," the pharmacist told him. "These things sometimes have dangerous side effects, especially in someone who's never taken them before. These drugs can make someone extremely happy, but vulnerable to temptation and doing things they wouldn't normally do. If the patient stops taking them abruptly, they can become extremely sad, violent, and even suicidal. Also they can become very addicting, even more so than street drugs."

Ted explained about the counselor giving the pills to his wife, and how Claudia had become violent and hateful.

"Are these things illegal?" Ted asked.

"If the therapist is licensed to prescribe, I'm afraid not, especially if you wife is taking them voluntarily."

Ted left with the information. When he got home, Claudia was gone. He noticed a note on the kitchen table.

"Ted, I can't stand it here with you. I'm staying at a shelter that Ann Ritz recommended. She has saved me from you. I won't be back for a few days."

Ted sat in front of the TV and stared at the note for hours. His wife was falling apart right before his eyes, and it seemed there wasn't a thing he could do.

"Why are you doing this Ann Ritz? Why?" He shouted at the TV when her commercial came on. "You won't take her away from me! I'm not giving up; Claudia's worth fighting for!"

Ted thought back to the custody battle, when he never thought they would get Tommy, but they did. He figured if he stuck this out, he could get Claudia back to normal.

The next day, the phone and electric bills came, and Ted got out the checkbook to pay them. He realized three thousand dollars had been withdrawn from the savings account. He knew exactly who had taken it out, and what she'd done with it. Just then Claudia came in. Her clothes were dirty, her eyes bloodshot.

"Claudia, um, listen, we need to chat," Ted said.

"I've just come to get a few things, then I'm leaving again," Claudia interrupted.

"Claudia! Those pills you're taking are making you act this way! That counselor is unprofessional and she's getting rich off ruining you. I love you, and I'm gonna help you got through this, whether you like it or not."

"Oh, now you're going through my stuff, too, ya son of a bitch!" Claudia screamed.

"Only 'cause I love you. We can beat this, we can beat Ann Ritz. I don't care about the money you wasted, or how much it'll cost to get you back."

Ted came closer to Claudia with his arms open and she backed away.

"Come on, I'll take you to a real doctor, he'll do what's right," Ted pleaded.

Claudia pulled out a knife as Ted came closer. Ted jumped back as she wildly aimed it at him.

"Jesus Christ! What's wrong with you?" Ted shouted.

"You will not stop me, Ted. You better use your gun, or get out of my way!" Claudia said.

Her hands were trembling as she held the knife, then she stormed off to get her stuff. Ted was forced to watch in horror as she packed and drove away. Ted remembered his gun, since Claudia mentioned it. It was a .45 handgun. He went to the closet to dig it out, then put some bullets in it and played with it for a while. Role-playing with it, he thought he was John Wayne in the Old West.

"All right, Ann, let's see who's quicker on the draw," Ted said out loud.

He put the gun away, drove to Ann's office. She was very busy with other clients, but he wanted to wait till they were gone. Ted noticed a new Honda with temp tags on it. Since he was a car guy, he valued the car at twenty thousand dollars and wondered if it belonged to Ann.

He went to the convenience store to buy Lucky Strike cigarettes. He hadn't smoked since he was a teenager, but found it helped pass time and relax him during these hard times. He waited outside Ann's office building till she's done with clients, even though it was over an hour. When he went inside, he didn't even put out the cigarette.

"What are you doing here?" Ann asked.

"Tell me what you want," Ted said.

"What do you mean?"

"How much money is it gonna take to get you to stay the hell away from my wife?"

"I want you to leave now," was all she said.

"Stay away, or you'll be sorry," Ted said, keeping his voice calm. "She's my wife and you will not ruin it for me. I have worked my whole fucking life away to get where I am today. Let me tell ya, some stupid hippie bitch like you isn't gonna take it away from me. You're a fraud. You don't know shit about counseling. All you know how to do is turn people into junkies!"

Ann picked up the phone and began to dial it.

"I'm calling the police," she said.

"Forget it, I'll leave," Ted said, realizing she was serious. "But don't forget what I said."

He looked at her with the most severe look Ann had ever seen. His wide psychotic eyes made her more than a little nervous, and she froze with the telephone in her hand. Ted walked out the door. Ann put the phone down and continued on with her business.

At work the next day, Ted was doing even worse. During his fifteen-minute break, he stared at the break-room table for an hour. Some of the young guys, below Ted, came in and joined him.

"Hey, Teddy, did that new girl Angela say something to you about me?" one of them asked.

Ted was upset and didn't want to deal with a bunch of stupid kids.

"Teddy? Who the hell's Teddy? Around here, I'm Mr. Amichi, you got that?" Ted said to them.

"Sorry, dude, but what did she say to you?"

"She said that you're staring at her too much. Now, I'm telling you to knock it off or you'll be fired."

"That bitch, it's only 'cause she wants me so bad. She wants to suck my dick. What do you think, Mr. Amichi, sir?" the kid said.

Usually Ted could blow this kind of thing off and humor them with lies and bullshit. Today he couldn't do it. He stood up and headed to the door.

"Kids, if you'll excuse me, I'm gonna see if I can find the grownups' break-room Bye."

The kids followed him out the door.

"Come on, dude, don't be such a hard on. What, are you having problems with your woman?"

Ted stopped walking, turned around fast to look at them.

"What did you say?" Ted said in tired voice.

"We can tell, and we can help ya."

"Yeah, sure, whatever, just go away," Ted said.

"Dude, listen..."

"Quit calling me dude!" Ted interrupted.

"Sorry, sir, but we can help you."

"How?"

"We can hook you up with someone; she's about your age.

"It doesn't work that way."

"Sure, it does; they're always another woman out there."

"I have been married to my wife twenty years; I'm not interested in your offer."

Ted was getting annoyed with these kids. He could tell them to leave and they would have to, but he was so desperate for help, he listened anyway.

"My buddy Ricky was engaged to a girl for over two years," the kid said. "He even got her pregnant, and when she dumped him, he went out and found one that looked just like her. It could be the same for you, man."

"Listen, I have to go."

Ted walked away, hoping they would stop him and give him more advice. But the kids thought he really didn't want help, so they went away.

Ted's production was down, and the kids weren't the only ones he snapped at. Claudia had been gone for three weeks when he came home from work and noticed things missing. Another two thousand dollars had been withdrawn from the savings account. He couldn't prevent Claudia from emptying the account unless he did first. Ann Ritz had made seven thousand dollars from Claudia in the last four months.

On June 3, 1999, Ted was at work, once again not feeling well, hung-over and smoking two packs of Lucky Strike cigarettes a day. The county sheriff showed up asking for Theodore Amichi.

"That's me."

The sheriff handed him papers. "I'm sorry, sir, but you've been served."

Ted stared at the papers. Sure enough, they were divorce papers from Claudia. The phone in his office rang, but he didn't answer it. The papers indicated that he was not allowed to contact Claudia, and he had thirty days to move out of the house.

All he would have left was the job and an old beat up '76 Cadillac. Ted felt so embarrassed. Everyone was staring at him.

Over the next week, he moved out some of his stuff, including the .45 handgun. He had to move into a cheap hotel in the inner-city of Detroit called The Detroit Inn. He stayed in Room 123. The first thing he noticed was the awful smell. It only took him twenty minutes to see that there were dirty diapers between the mattress and box spring of the bed. Ted went to wash his hands in the bathroom. He noticed dead cockroaches floating in the toilet.

Chapter 15

Finding Ann

Somehow, Ted got through the period until the court date. Claudia was awarded the house, the newer car, and what few pennies were left in the savings account. Since Tommy was grown up, nobody had to pay child support, and there was no alimony. The '76 Cadillac was not in shape to be used full time, but it was all Ted had left. He didn't have the money to even go out drinking anymore, nor was he allowed to see Claudia. He only worked and went home to a small, crappy hotel room located right in the ghetto of the city. Ted missed Claudia so much, but he still couldn't even sleep with the many hookers that were around his hotel.

One day at work, the president asked Ted to come to his office. Benny Stone (the man who'd hired Ted) had retired. His son, Benny Junior, was in charge.

"What is it, sir?" Ted asked.

"Ted, we've noticed your incompetence and slacking on the job. Also, we've lost a few accounts because of your rudeness. Last but not least, employees are filing grievances against you," Benny said.

"Well, things have been tough, but you're right; I'll get back on the ball," Ted said in a worried voice.

"Ted, save the explanations; I've decided to terminate you from GM."

"What? Now, wait. Your father hired me himself. We've gone through tough times together, and I can't say goodbye now."

"My father's gone; I'm here and I don't want you here."

"Now, I don't think you understand..." Ted said heatedly.

"I do understand, and my decision is final."

"My wife divorced me; it's been rough. That's why I've been down, but now it's over and I'm ready to go back to my old self," Ted said so loud it could be heard outside the office.

"Sorry, Ted."

Benny stood up, ready to show Ted out the door, and put his hand on Ted's arm. It was the last straw.

"Get your hands off me!" Ted yelled.

"Then go," Benny said. "I'll mail your last paycheck to you in a week."

Not knowing what else to do, Ted got up and left. He hadn't been alone or without a job in over twenty years. The Cadillac needed a new carburetor, but he couldn't afford one. He got in his car, drove over to Ann Ritz's office. All he was planning to do was give her a big sarcastic "Thank you for ruining my life!" But when he got there, the place was empty with a "For Lease" sign on the door. Ted went to the office next door.

"Do you know what happened to the shrink who used to be next door?" Ted asked.

"Nope," they said. "We just saw movers here a couple of days ago. We don't know where they went."

He drove to the old Barney's for a few drinks. He saw Charlie, whom he hadn't seen in years. Charlie was tired, hung-over, dirty and looked even worse than Ted.

"Charlie Fletcher, that you?" Ted said.

"Oh, my God, Ted -! Wow, man, it's been a while," Charlie said.

"Yep, do you want to go the junkyard with me? I need to find a good used carburetor."

"Oh, man, you still driving this old beast? I thought you had a newer one."

"I'll explain on the way," Ted said. They left the bar to go to the junkyard.

"Well, Ted I hope you and Claudia have done better in your marriage than I did."

Ted was surprised; last he remembered, Charlie was doing quite well in life.

"What do you mean?" Ted asked.

"My wife divorced me, and took all my stuff," Charlie said.

"Really! Why?"

"We were having problems, but they were only small ones. So we decided to go see this marriage counselor. Next thing I knew, my baby hated me and left," Charlie said.

"This counselor, her name wouldn't happen to be Ann Ritz?"

Ted felt it was just a shot in the dark. No way in the world they were both screwed by the same counselor.

"Have you been stalking me, Teddy?" Charlie asked.

"What?"

"How'd you know it was Ann Ritz?"

"Jesus Christ! My wife left me too after we saw Ann Ritz."

"What? Oh, man, how'd she do it?" Charlie asked.

"I found out my wife was taking these expensive pills that Ann prescribed. The influence of her so-called 'counseling' and the pills took my baby Claudia away from me."

"I'll bet my wife was on those same pills," Charlie said. "I noticed she was taking pills in the morning, but she told me they were for her allergies."

"Oh, did I mention Claudia also took my house, my newer car, and all the money, I worked for so many years to save up?" Ted said. "It'll probably end up going to Ann Ritz."

"God, why would Claudia leave you? She was crazy about you," Charlie said.

"So she could marry Ann Ritz and give her all my money," Ted replied sarcastically.

"Most of my stuff was taken, too."

"Oh, and did I also mention that because of the stress of losing Claudia, I lost my job at GM?"

"No shit. So I guess that's why you're driving this old car, huh?"

"Yep." They arrived at the junkyard, with the car overheating.

"Hey, Ted, I can't get out!"

"Oh, yeah, you have to roll down the window and open it from the outside, 'cause the handle broke." They looked around the junkyard at the old Cadillacs.

"My God, I remember when all these old cars were brand-new," Ted said.

"Yeah, you probably built most of these."

"Yep, and I was young, happy, and new. Now, just like these cars, I'm old and in the junkyard waiting to die or be crushed."

"If it hadn't been for Ann Ritz, I could have fixed the marriage problems," Charlie said.

"Hell, mine didn't have any problems. We just wanted to see Ann for the hell of it. Well, wait! Correction, Claudia wanted to see her; I knew she was trouble when I saw her on TV."

"Yep." Charlie took out a bottle of Old Crow scotch from his coat pocket and had a few swigs.

"Want some, Teddy?" Ted took the bottle without answering and had a few swigs too.

"Goddamnit, if I had just said 'no' to Claudia. It would have made her mad that day, but by now she'd have been over it and still be with me," Ted said as he took the carburetor off one of the old cars he'd found.

"I know; but what's done is done, Ted."

"Ann's office was always busy. If she got as much money out of everyone else as she did out of me and Claudia, she has to be loaded."

"We should go pay her a little visit today," Charlie said.

"Can't. She left; her office is as empty as my heart."

"Fuck! Where'd she go?" Charlie asked.

"Fuck if I know."

Ted finished taking off the carburetor and paid the junkyard owner. Ted and Charlie went back to Ted's hotel to look through the telephone books.

"There's tons of Ritze's in the book. If she's married, it wouldn't even be in her name," Ted said.

"I wouldn't be surprised if she left the state," Charlie added.

Over the next week, Charlie moved into Ted's hotel to help pay the rent. They both took turns visiting Ann Ritz's former office to see what was happening. On a late Thursday afternoon, Ted went down there alone. The doors were open; he saw a crew remodeling the place. Ted felt sad being in the place where his life had started falling to pieces.

"This is where it all happened, because of you Ann Ritz, wherever the hell you are," Ted said to himself.

The mailman arrived, shoving some letters through the mail slot. The work crew wasn't paying attention, so Ted went snooping through the mail. Most of it was bills or junk mail. A handwritten letter got Ted's attention. It said "Peggy Reddick" on it. The return address said nothing more than "Omaha, Nebraska." Even the postmark said Omaha, NE. Since no one knew him or was even paying attention, Ted put the letter in his coat. When he got home, Charlie was there, sitting at the table drinking scotch and playing solitaire.

"I went to Ann's place; the doors were open, and the mail man came. He dropped off this letter to a Peggy Reddick," Ted said as he showed Charlie the letter.

"I can't believe you just took it," Charlie said, clearing a place on the table for Ted.

"Nobody saw me."

"Who's Peggy Reddick?" Charlie asked.

"I don't know; maybe it's the landlord, or Ann's real name."

"Maybe, God knows if my last name was Red Dick, I'd change it."

"No, I don't think that's why. It's probably so when she closes up shop nobody will be able to track her down. Don't tell me I'm the only one who's after her. Heck, I bet the law would like a word with her as well. "

"Well, we can track her down," Charlie said with a laugh.

Ted opened the letter carefully, so it can be resealed without anyone knowing he'd opened it. It took more than ten minutes to open the envelope, but finally he did it. There was a letter inside. Neither Ted nor Charlie could wait to see it. It said:

"Dear Peggy, hope you're doing well out there. Your husband's getting really suspicious about why you're always out shopping when he calls here. I hope to see you before you head back home." The bottom of the letter said: "From the Nebraska crew."

"Hmm, no names on who these folks are in Nebraska," Ted said.

"I wonder what they meant by the husband was suspicious?" Charlie asked.

"Well, it still doesn't tell us where she is."

"Wait, what about a forwarding address?"

"Yeah, the post office might know if she left a forwarding address for little Miss Lying Peggy Reddick."

"They're not gonna tell you what it is. They'll just send the letter to her," Charlie said.

"I don't know; maybe I can talk 'em into it somehow," Ted said.

"Good luck; that's the federal government you're dealing with."

That night Ted stayed up thinking of how he was going to get the post office to give him Peggy's forwarding address. By morning, he'd thought of a way, but didn't have much confidence in it. He resealed the envelope. It looked like it had never been opened at all. Ted went to the post office. He took a deep breath before he entered the front door, knowing he only had one chance to get the address out of them; failure was not an option.

On the way inside, he saw a sign that said: "Help Wanted." It took Ted a moment to realize it, but he decided to put the letter in his pocket and abandon his first plan. Instead, he asked the post office clerk for an application.

"We're looking for mail separators and clerks," the women said.

"How much does clerk pay?" Ted asked.

"Only eight dollars an hour, but it can help you get a better job later."

"That'll be great; I need all I can get."

He filled out the application. The post office needed clerks so badly the process only took two weeks to get Ted hired. Ted learned how to weigh letters and greet and help customers. It only took a few days to learn the job completely. After six days on the job, Ted was ready to try his new plan. While helping a customer who needed a box sent to New York, Ted was rehearsing what to say. He put the right stamps on, told the customer to have a great day, then went to find the supervisor.

"Hey, Will, this guy brought this letter in and said it needs to be forwarded. How do we do that?" Ted said as he pulled out the letter to Peggy Reddick.

"Come here, I'll show you." Ted followed Will, realizing this might work out.

"We look up the person's name and old address, to see if they left a forwarding address." They looked up Peggy.

"Now, look here. See, Peggy Reddick has a forwarding address," Will said.

Ted looked at Peggy's address. It showed she lives in a small town in Utah; he memorized the address.

"Thank you, sir," Ted said.

"Oh, and one more thing, never give the actual address out to anyone. Especially if it is protected, like Peggy Reddick's is."

The computer did show that Peggy had her forwarding address protected. Ted knew his old plan could never have worked. For that moment, he felt on top of the world again, outsmarting the system and outsmarting Peggy. For the rest of the day, Ted was in a great mood. Peggy had done so much to protect her real identity, but it wasn't enough to stop Ted, not even close. After work, Ted met Charlie at the hotel.

"Wanna go on a road trip?" Charlie asked Ted when he heard what Ted had done.

"Sure." Ted and Charlie looked at each other.

"Look, Ted, why don't we take three days and think about whether we really want to do this," Charlie said, changing his mind.

"Okay, three days." Over the next three days, Ted and Charlie thought about it. They met after work.

"Well, I've thought about it," Ted said.

"Yeah, me, too."

"I have nothing, so I can lose nothing."

"That's exactly what I thought," Charlie said.

"Are you sure you wanna do this with me, Charlie?"

"Yep."

Ted and Charlie looked at each other, then went and packed up for the road trip. Charlie got some clothes and gas money. Ted got clothes, food, gas money, and his .45.

"Since I've had so much time on my hands, I decided to spruce up the old Caddy," Ted said.

"What did you do to it?"

"Well, years ago, I borrowed--well, okay, stole--some of those illegal tires for my Caddy."

"Why illegal?"

"They're solid rubber, and not even a rifle-shot can flatten these bad boys. They were banned for sale, but I was able to get a few. Also, I got a high-performance transmission that fits really well."

"Wow this old Caddy's bad-ass," Charlie said.

They got in the Cadillac. Before hitting the Interstate, they drove around the city to say goodbye to the place both had spent the best part of their lives in. The road trip took two days. When they arrived in the small town, they were both relieved.

"This is a pretty creepy town," Charlie said.

They stopped at a gas station, and Charlie bought a city roadmap. They found their way to Peggy's part of town, only to realize they couldn't get in there.

"Aw, look, she lives in one of those gated communities," Charlie said.

"Oh, man, there's an armed guard at the entrance gates!" Ted replied. A twelve-foot tall brick wall fenced in the whole neighborhood.

"How are we gonna get to her house?" Charlie asked.

"I don't know; we can't climb the wall. The guards will call the cops or shoot us if we drive through the gates."

Ted and Charlie drove away to look around the little town. They stopped at a pay phone, and took the White Pages out of it. They looked up Reddick. The name in the book that matched the address was Jack Reddick.

"Okay, let's think," Ted said. "How are we gonna talk to Peggy if we can't get into her housing development?"

"The only way would be to get her outside the house, like at work or something," Charlie said.

"How are we gonna know where she works?"

"Tomorrow we'll wait outside the gates until she comes out and follow her."

They agreed, and drove around for a while. It was 3:00 P.M.; being bored they found an Italian market and deli in the small town and decided to go in. It looked just like an authentic New York Italian deli.

"Hey, may I a help you?" the man behind the counter said in an Eastern accent.

The two guys introduced themselves as the owners. One was tall and muscular with gray hair; the other was short and overweight with no hair and a really strong accent. Ted and Charlie ordered sandwiches.

"Wow, is that your Cadillac?" the short one asked, admiring it through the window.

"Yep," Ted replied.

The two men went on to tell about their restaurant. Ted tried to pay attention, but couldn't help wondering how surprised Peggy would be when she saw him. The guys were ultra-polite; little did they know what Ted and Charlie were doing there. Ted and Charlie ate, then left.

"I hope you come back real soon," the tall man said.

Although the deli was a nice place, the rest of the town was boring, and many years behind in technology. Ted and Charlie could feel a chill that no cold air could ever cause. They didn't know if it was the town being small and boring, or if it was that they were just so used to the big city. They stopped at a chain store in town to buy a scanner codebook for the police scanner Ted had brought along. He typed in the scanner code for the local city police, the county sheriff's department and the Utah State Patrol.

"Now we can monitor where the cops are, in case we get them called on us," Ted said.

The next morning at 5:30 A.M., Ted and Charlie parked across the street from Peggy's gated community. They waited till 6:00 A.M., but Peggy didn't come out. Seven o'clock came, but still no sign of Peggy. The sun was starting to come up and Ted and Charlie were tired of waiting. Ted walked down the block to a doughnut shop to got two cups of coffee and a dozen doughnuts. When he got back,

Charlie seemed in a daze from waiting so long. Ted handed him the coffee.

"Hey, Ted, what if she doesn't go to work until noon or something?" Charlie asked.

"Well, then you better get comfortable, because we aren't leaving till her car comes out those gates."

"Shit, I'm surprised we haven't been arrested yet," Charlie said.

A car came through the gates. It looked like the car Peggy had driven when she was in Detroit. Ted got out the binoculars. While the guard was validating her card, Ted stared at her through the lenses.

"Is that her?" Charlie asked.

"Yep."

Ted started the car, and let Peggy get far ahead of him so she wouldn't get suspicious. She pulled up at the local middle school, parked in the teachers' parking lot, then went inside.

"How do you like that? She works for the school," Ted said.

They drove away from the school, hoping nobody had seen them.

"I get to go inside and see where she is and what she does," Charlie said.

Charlie got out some old clothes and a baseball hat. They drove back to the school.

"Do I look like a janitor? Or at least close?" Charlie asked.

"As close as we're gonna get."

Charlie didn't go in the main entrance, but to a side door instead. He found the nearest broom closet and got out a janitor's cart. The cart had a broom, a trashcan, and many cleaning agents on it. Charlie looked real as he wheeled the cart around the school. He peeped in every classroom, but didn't see Peggy. Thinking he'd missed her, he checked the rooms again. Nothing. He went to the teachers' lounge, on the way to the main office. She wasn't there, either.

"Hey you, janitor! Can we get help? We had a wet spill in the counseling office," a voice said. Charlie was far away, at the other end of the hall.

"Be right there!" he said without looking at the person.

After a moment he looked, then looked twice, but there was no doubt it was Peggy who had called him. Charlie went to the counseling office. The sign on the door said "Mrs. Reddick: Counseling." Charlie looked behind him to see Peggy coming toward him.

"I need to get more rags," Charlie said to the counseling office secretary.

"Okay," she replied.

Charlie went the opposite way from Peggy, eventually making it outside the school. He found Ted in the parking lot across the street.

"Ted, you're not going to believe this--she's the goddamn school counselor!" Charlie said in a frantic voice.

"Oh, great! I'll bet she tells all the girls to dump their high school sweethearts. Well, tomorrow we're gonna pay her a little visit," Ted said.

That night Ted and Charlie worked on the Cadillac, adding several upgrade items. They put on nitrous boosters, and made sure the high-performance transmission Ted had built back in Detroit was still in good working order. He took off the license plates, and anything on the car that had the VIN numbers, and burned them along with the registration. There was no way the car could ever be traced to him or Charlie.

The next day, November 8, 1999, Ted and Charlie stopped at a local pawnshop.

"I guess I don't need this anymore," Charlie said as he took off his wedding ring.

Chapter 16

Ted's Story Ends

"That's it, everyone," Ted finished his story in the courtroom. "Next thing I knew, I was killing Peggy with my .45."

Jack, Andy, Nita and Ted's lawyer Mary were all still sitting quietly. They were a bit tired from listening to the story for over two hours.

"So as you can see, Your Honor, I had a motive," Ted said.

"Obviously," Judge Foster said dryly. "And I see no remorse for the pain you have caused Mr. Reddick and his family. What about Officer Marshall?"

"Now, that was just an accident," Ted replied.

Nita looked at Ted with her teary eyes. She didn't feel bad for Ted, but was saddened by his story.

"I've weighed all the facts," Foster said. "And I have reached a verdict."

Ted and Charlie looked directly at the judge, realizing what he was going to say.

"Theodore Amichi and Charlie Fletcher, you have been found guilty of two counts of first-degree murder. The penalty is death by firing squad."

Everyone was appalled by the verdict. Ted and Charlie were taken away in cuffs. Jack couldn't see the look on Ted's face when the judge said the word "death."

Chapter 17

Jack's Recovery

Jack left the courtroom with his two grown kids on either side of him. Ted and Charlie's appeals would take years to complete.

Over the first year, Jack had a tough reality to face. He'd always thought, through the years, that once the men were gone, it would be over and his life would get back to normal. In many Hollywood movies, everyone lives happily ever after once the murderers were sentenced to death. In Jack's life, it wasn't even close. His wife was still dead; his kids were grown and hardly knew their father. The verdict brought no relief. Jack thought about what would've happened if he'd never spent any time finding Ted and Charlie. They might not be on Death Row now, but his kids would never have had to suffer so much. Jack realized too late that over that first year his own life should've been more important than Ted's. He could've raised the children right instead of hunting Ted down. Eventually, Ted would've died anyway; he and his kids could've had a somewhat decent life. It wouldn't have been the way it was before, but it would have been much better than it was now. Jack never actually said he regretted finding Ted, but the question was constantly on his mind.

One year after Ted's sentencing, Jack thought his life was over. This case had become his life; without it, he was nothing. Who was Jack Reddick if he was not the man hunting his wife's killer? Work was boring, the kids were distant and he was almost fifty. All he had was debt, emotionally disturbed kids, and his dead wife. At least during the chasing years he had had hope; hope that once the murderers were gone, life would be back to normal.

Without even realizing it, Jack knew he and Ted were the same. Ted thought once Peggy was dead, his life would be back to the way it was. He'd found out otherwise. Jack and Ted had both lost their wives, and thought that killing someone would bring them back.

At least it wasn't completely over for Jack. Now that a year had gone by since the sentencing, he thought it might not be too late for he and his kids to get back together. Over the next couple of years Jack did what he could to cheer up his kids. They were both almost adults, but it didn't matter. The kids felt better now that their dad was going back to the way he was. His daughter Nita was nineteen. Jack encouraged her to start liking cartoons and kid stuff again, the way she did before this big mess. One day, Jack saw Nita looking gloomy on the way home from college. Even though it was chilly out, she wasn't wearing her Garfield coat.

"What's wrong?" Jack asked her.

"A girl at school told me I shouldn't wear my Garfield coat, because that's for kids."

"Who cares? Wear what you like. You don't have to be grown up now. You can be a kid now, because you never got to be a kid growing up, because of Ted," Jack said. Nita smiled and put the coat right back on.

"Dad, this Thursday was the school play. You're coming, right?" Nita asked.

"You know I'll be there. Which one of the Cinderella characters are you playing?"

"One of her evil sisters. If I do well, my drama teacher said I could get the main role in Romeo and Juliet next semester." Andy came home, just as they finished talking.

"Hey, Andy, did you get those worms for our fishing trip tomorrow?" Jack asked.

"Yep, but I still say we should use fake worms."

"Now, son, let me tell ya, the fish can tell the difference."

Jack went fishing with Andy for the whole weekend. The two of them hadn't been fishing in so long that they have to learn all over again. On a weekend in late January, they went skiing in Colorado. Jack didn't even look at anyone along the way, and only stopped for gas. All of them enjoyed the trip, not once thinking of Ted. Although the three of them would never forget Peggy, they were able to cope and move on.

Ironically, the healing hadn't started until Ted and Charlie were sentenced to death. Jack realized that it wasn't the sentence that began the healing. It was his realizing that the fate of the murderers didn't matter.

On Nita's 22nd birthday, Jack felt he'd made up for all the neglected years. In the last three years he had spent every weekend doing something with the kids. They have traveled the county, looking at natural landmarks and museums. They've been to Washing D. C. and almost met the President face to face. They didn't always spend money; just spending time together was loads of fun. During the winter months, Jack took them skiing at least once a month. He even volunteered at Andy's high school when he could. Even if he had to take off work, he did. Although he was in a lot of debt from the trial, the vacations and taking time off work, he didn't care. Money could be re-earned, but he felt that he'd gotten his kids back, and truly defeated Ted. Nita and Andy were both dating. They were both proud to call Jack "Dad" again. They both acted mature in most ways, yet in others they were like little happy kids again.

On the seventh anniversary of Peggy's death, Jack dreamed of her. Peggy was smiling at him for once. This was the first time she had smiled in any of his dreams of her. Most of his dreams lately were about his job, and hardly any of Ted anymore.

About halfway into the year, Jack received a letter from the state correctional facility. Inside were three passes. The letter explained that Ted and Charlie's appeals had run out, and they were going to be executed in one month. The passes were for Jack and the kids to watch the execution live. Jack showed the letter to the kids, and they all agreed to go.

After eight and a half years, this was supposed to be the day Jack had been waiting for -- the mission, the reason for living, the only reward he ever wanted in life. The man who murdered his wife was finally going to die. Instead, Jack hardly thought about it. Other dates, like Nita's graduation from college and Andy's wedding, were more important.

The day finally arrived. The execution would be at 7:30 P.M. The sun was setting over the hills when Jack and his kids entered the prison. Jack took a seat and begins to think. He first thought was of how much better his life was now than it had been a few years ago when Ted's trial started. It was not back to the way things were before this mess, but it was okay now. He thought about the day Peggy died.

"If I only knew what was going to happen that day," Jack said.

He wasn't so much referring to Peggy's murder, but to what years of agony he was going to put himself through to catch the two killers. He also thought about when he was in jail for three days. He had hit rock bottom back then, but he could actually laugh about it now.

"How could I be so foolish as to get myself put in jail because of these guys?" Jack said to the kids.

As Ted was being brought out in chains, he had a lot to think about too. Looking at Jack and his kids, he realized he could have been like Jack. Things would never have been the way they were before Peggy, but they might've been okay, like they were for Jack now.

Through the years, Jack had always thought he would be cheering and hollering on the execution day of his wife's killer. But now he wasn't; instead he was calm and wanted to watch, just for the heck of it. He didn't even have any signs that said: "Hey Ted, you're dead." He didn't give Ted a dirty look when he came into the chamber. If Ted were to get a last minute stay of execution, it wouldn't even matter to Jack.

Both Ted and Jack have learned a lot from each other. Even though they're on different sides of the chamber, they're truly the same. According to the letter, Charlie would be executed in a few weeks. The guards strapped Ted to the chair and the shooters loaded their guns.

"Theodore Amichi, you've been condemned to die. Do you have anything to say before sentence is carried out?" the guard said.

"There's nothing I can say that will make a difference," Ted said.

"I hope if there's an afterlife, that Ted and Charlie won't make the same mistake again," Jack said to his kids.

Jack realized at that moment how lucky he was. He was getting a second chance, but Ted wasn't.

Ted's final thoughts were of Claudia. He remembered their wedding day and how good he'd felt. He remembered when she was walking up the aisle to him. He knew he would never forget her walking towards him, but never knew it would be the last thing he thought of.

"Ready..." the executioner said sharply. "Aim..."

The five shooters aimed their guns at Ted, who was still thinking of his wedding day. Claudia had been so beautiful. The days were bright, and he remembered how happy he was. He remembered when they finally got custody of Tommy, and he remembered his second honeymoon in Vegas.

I felt such virtue toward life, Ted thought. Even though he'd had it all back then, he didn't have the knowledge he had now about how to handle a bad situation. He wished he could look at Claudia's beautiful face again. He didn't even know where she was, and hadn't seen her in years. Last he had heard, Tommy was married and doing fine; Claudia had entered the emergency room for a heart attack. On the other hand, he was glad she wasn't here. He didn't want his darling wife to see him this way. Instead of crying, Ted smiled as he thought of Claudia and his good times over the years. He thought he'd learned what he needed to learn in this life. He hoped there was an afterlife, so he could try again. He hoped to marry someone as good as Claudia and have a son like Tommy.

Once again, he thought of Claudia walking towards him on their wedding day. God, she was so beautiful -- the best wife any man could ever want.

He heard the executioner yell: "FIRE!"

DID YOU ENJOY THIS BOOK?

SEND QUESTIONS OR COMMENTS TO THE AUTHOR:

DAVE AQUINO
P.O. BOX 741351
ARVADA, CO 80006-1351

Books by Dave Aquino

Personal War

Personal War Part 2

Counselor

The Slot Machine